This is what they've

On #143 *LIFE LINE:*

"Fasten your seat belts. Rebecca York takes you on a thrilling trip into the shadowy world of mystery and suspense and the steamy world of romance."+

On #155 *SHATTERED VOWS:*

"Superlative suspense that will make the hairs on the back of your neck…scream for help…a strong love story to win your heart."†

On #167 *WHISPERS IN THE NIGHT:*

"York makes you think twice about turning out the lights, in this masterfully plotted novel of romantic suspense."†

On #179 *ONLY SKIN DEEP:*

"Another hellraiser! The tension is at a fever pitch, with a strong romance and a cunning mystery."†

On #193 *TRIAL BY FIRE:*

"A mind-blowing concoction of black magic and timeless romance that will fire your imagination and sear your soul!"†

On #213 *HOPSCOTCH:*

"An electrifying foray into hi-tech skullduggery and sizzling romance!"†

On #233 *CRADLE AND ALL:*

"A superlative foray into heartstopping suspense, daring adventure and uplifting romance."†

On #253 *WHAT CHILD IS THIS?:*

"Chilling suspense and snowballing excitement from a master of intrigue."†

+Alberta Ferguson, Alberta's Book Service
†*Romantic Times*

Directory
4 3 L I G H T S T R E E T

	Room
ADVENTURES IN TRAVEL	204
ABIGAIL FRANKLIN, Ph.D. Clinical Psychology	509
INNER HARBOR PRODUCTIONS	101
THE LIGHT STREET FOUNDATION	322
KATHRYN MARTIN-McQUADE, M.D. Branch Office, Medizone Labs	515
O'MALLEY & O'MALLEY Detective Agency	518
LAURA ROSWELL, LL.B. Attorney at Law	311
SABRINA'S FANCY	Lobby
STRUCTURAL DESIGN GROUP	407
NOEL ZACHARIAS Paralegal Service	311
L. ROSSINI Superintendent	Lower Level

ABOUT THE AUTHOR

Cowriters and friends, Ruth Glick and Eileen Buckholtz created the Rebecca York pseudonym years ago and have built it into one of the most recognizable names in romantic suspense. Between them, they've written over sixty books, including romance, suspense, young-adult fiction and even cookbooks. Called a "true master of intrigue," Rebecca York is the winner of the *Romantic Times* Career Achievement Award for Romantic Mystery and was a RITA Award finalist in 1992 for best romantic suspense of the year. Both Ruth and Eileen, and their respective families, live in Maryland.

Books by Rebecca York

HARLEQUIN INTRIGUE
143—LIFE LINE*
155—SHATTERED VOWS*
167—WHISPERS IN THE NIGHT*
179—ONLY SKIN DEEP*
188—BAYOU MOON
193—TRIAL BY FIRE*
213—HOPSCOTCH*
233—CRADLE AND ALL*
253—WHAT CHILD IS THIS?*
273—MIDNIGHT KISS*

*43 Light Street titles

Chapter One

Jo O'Malley crouched behind a rusted telephone transformer box, hands clenched tightly on her camera case, a cap pulled low over her red curls. When the man she'd been following stepped through the door again, she was going to be ready. She'd already missed a couple of possible shots because he'd turned too quickly. Soon there wouldn't be enough light to get his face.

The seconds ticked by, and she shifted uncomfortably, feeling sharp gravel dig into her knees. Just when she thought her body would snap like a dry twig if she didn't change her position, the door opened. Carefully she adjusted the telephoto lens, focusing on her subject's face. It was ugly. Like a reptile. If he cracked his lips, would a forked tongue flick out?

She squeezed off six shots in rapid succession as he descended the short flight of stairs from the loading dock.

When he turned the corner, she hesitated. She wanted more evidence, but it would be foolish to press her luck. Instead, she waited to make sure her quarry wasn't doubling back in her direction. Then she pushed herself up and stretched the kinks out of her muscles before starting back toward the silver Lexus.

Now that she was no longer focused on the man, she was suddenly aware of her isolation. A cold wind was blowing off the Patapsco River, and she struggled to repress a little shiver. Coming to the warehouse district by herself wasn't the swiftest move in the world, but there wasn't anyone else she could trust—particularly not her husband. Staying in the shadows of the red-brick buildings, she kept her senses tuned to her surroundings. But the only footsteps she detected were her own; the only movement was the wind toying with the trash strewn across the cracked cement.

Her car had picked this morning to conk out, so she'd borrowed one of Cameron's. It was stashed behind a Dumpster, where it ought to be okay.

As she spotted the vehicle, she felt a pang of guilt. She'd told Cam she was on an insurance investigation. Which wasn't exactly a lie, if you stretched the definition of insurance a little bit.

Fumbling in her purse, she pulled out the special remote control that deactivated the car's alarm. The system was something Randolph Electronics—Cam's company—had in development, but it wouldn't be on the market until they brought the price down from the thousand- to the hundred-dollar range.

As Jo pressed a series of codes, the red light on the controller changed to green. After slipping behind the wheel and locking the door, she breathed a little sigh of relief and tossed her cap into the back seat. She was safe.

The car's cellular phone was equipped with another one of Randolph's exclusive features. She could see from the liquid crystal display that someone had tried to reach her. Her home number flashed on the little screen when she hit the Recall button. After starting the engine, she pressed the automatic dialer.

Cam answered on the first ring. "Jo?"

His anxious tone made her stomach clench, but she tried to keep her own voice even as she quickly unloaded a film cartridge from her camera. "Hi."

"Dammit, Jo. It's after five. I was starting to worry. Where are you?"

"Everything's fine. I'm on my way home now." As she spoke, she set the film roll on the seat beside her and eased out of the parking space.

"Where are you?" he repeated.

"I'm sorry. My client wants to keep confidential," she said in a neutral tone, glad that he hadn't gotten around to installing one of his videophones in the car.

The noise of an engine made her look to the right, and she saw a van shoot out in front of the Lexus, blocking its path. With an indrawn gasp of surprise, she slammed on the brakes.

"Jo? What happened?"

"A van just blocked me in." Needing her full concentration, she dropped the phone onto the seat, gripped the wheel and threw the car into Reverse. It was already too late. A twin to the first van had pulled up in back of her, blocking the only escape route.

"Jo, for God's sake!" Her husband's voice seemed far away and close by at the same time.

"Help! Cam, help me."

"Jo. Jo."

Like an evil spirit blinking into existence, a man had appeared beside her door. A large man with a gun in his hand.

When he yanked on the handle, she reached for the weapon in her purse. She'd barely pulled it free when she heard an explosion and felt a hot pain slice into her chest.

Cam was still calling her, and she tried to say something to him, but a bubble of blood broke on her lips. The car door was supposed to be locked. Vaguely she wondered how it had opened. Then rough hands were dragging her from the car and dumping her onto the pavement.

She blinked, staring up at two hazy faces so far above her that if she stretched out her arm she'd never reach them.

"You moron. You killed her."

"She had a gun. It was either her or me."

"We'd better get out of here. Fast."

Her chest hurt. So much. She tried to get up, but her arms and legs wouldn't work.

Oh, Cam. I didn't tell you I loved you when I left the house this morning.

She was cold. Everything was fading...fading... fading to black. Even the pain was gone.

All at once she could see a soft amber glow shining in the dark, beckoning her forward. Tentatively she moved closer. Then she was rushing toward the brightness, not on her feet, but flying through the air. The light was at the beginning of a tunnel. A tunnel to peace and safety. And at the entrance she could see a figure waiting for her.

IT SOUNDED LIKE a shot! Cold, numbing terror coursed through Cameron Randolph's veins as he shouted into the telephone receiver. "Jo! Answer me!"

His wife didn't respond. Turning up the volume, he strained to hear what was happening. In the background he caught muffled voices, a curse, the reviving of an engine. Then the line went dead, and his heart stopped. It sped up in double time as agonizing seconds ticked by. A series of terrifying pictures flashed through his brain. Jo being dragged from the car; Jo in some deserted alley bleeding, dying. Worst of all, he didn't even know where the hell she was.

His frantic gaze swept around his home lab, searching for something—anything—he could use to pinpoint his wife's location. Ten million dollars' worth of technology that didn't add up to a bag of manure if it couldn't help him get Jo back alive and unharmed. He snatched up a spare keyboard and smashed it against the wall. The resounding crash brought back a measure of sanity.

Calm down. Think.

Running his fingers through his dark hair, he closed his eyes and concentrated on the facts he knew. Jo was driving her classic Mustang. No, that wasn't right. The damn thing had been in the shop again this morning, and she'd borrowed his Lexus. The one with the prototype cellular phone he'd been testing. And she'd taken the new two-way beeper, as well. That was his best bet. If she was wearing it. And if she was within range.

Let it work, he chanted over and over as he turned to the computer. With a series of quick commands, he instructed the device to send out a locater signal similar to the ones in the black boxes used to find airplane crash sites.

The screen flashed to life, and Cam waited breathlessly for the tracker to respond. All he got for his trouble was a message that said No Hits Found For Current Search. To Continue Enter New Parameters. A choice expletive exploded from his lips. Jo was too far away. That left the car phone. He didn't allow himself to think about the seconds of her life ticking away as he executed a new set of commands that signed him on to the cellular network. He wasn't authorized to nose around the usage logs, but he wasn't going to waste hours getting the proper permissions. Instead, he took advantage of a security glitch he'd found while evaluating their system and went directly to the encoded log of recent calls.

God, please don't let me be too late, he prayed. The green glow of the monitor reflected back the agonized lines of his face as he waited an eternity for the program to search the thousands of calls made every hour. In his mind, scenes from his three-year marriage to Jo flashed like clips from a video library. Their wedding, with his new bride kicking off her high heels halfway through the reception. Their honeymoon, when he'd chased her down that private stretch of Bermuda beach until she let him catch her and make love to her on the sand. Jo hiding a group of their friends down here in the lab to surprise him when he went down to work as usual on his birthday. Jo curled up beside him while they watched the old Hitchcock movies she loved. And then her eyes changing seductively from soft green to smoky blue as she turned in his arms and smiled. He had to blink away the moisture in his own eyes as he struggled to keep the screen from blurring into a green haze.

When the data base flashed Ready, his hand jumped on the keys. After swiping his sleeve across his face, he extracted the coordinates of the cell that had picked up Jo's call. With another keystroke, he superimposed the location on a map of Baltimore city and printed it.

South Baltimore. What kind of case was she wondering on this time? No wonder she hadn't told him where she was going. She knew he'd be worried out of his mind. He tore off the printout, scooped up his portable tracker and ran out the door.

Five minutes later he was on the beltway weaving his old Lotus in and out of traffic at seventy miles per hour, almost hoping he'd pick up a patrol car. Then he'd have a police escort. From his car phone, he called Dan Cassidy's home extension. An assistant state's attorney and a friend he'd met through Jo, Cassidy could mobilize the cops. But Dan wasn't home, his wife Sabrina told him. He'd gone to the office to finish up some work. Cam reached him there.

"Dan, Jo's been car jacked, but the vehicle's equipped with tracking equipment."

"Where is she?"

"South Baltimore—north Locus Point. She may have been shot. I'm probably twenty minutes away."

"We'll send some units into the area and put Shock Trauma on call, too," Dan promised. "What kind of vehicle are we looking for?"

"A 1994 gray Lexus, license number RAND01. As soon as I get her exact location, I'll call you back." After thanking Dan for his help, Cam hung up. As he maneuvered through the Saturday evening traffic, his eyes flicked to the tracker screen, and his ears strained for that first telltale beep. Why wasn't the blasted thing picking up the location? If it didn't register soon, he'd have to search street by street, alley by alley.

When the signal sounded, it was like a shot of some potent drug hitting his bloodstream. The next scan showed the homing device hadn't moved. That meant Jo was in one place—if the emitter wasn't simply lying on the ground somewhere.

He took the next ramp off I-95. Soon he was speeding through dark streets lined with abandoned buildings interspersed with a few grungy businesses.

Turning a corner, Cam careered into a vacant lot near the Patapsco River. The only illumination came from a single street lamp. No people. No cars. Just rundown warehouses. Slowing his speed to a crawl, he got back to Dan with his location. His eyes probed the shadows as he adjusted the settings on the tracker from broad to sensitive scan. It was a little like playing the you're-getting-warmer-or-colder game. Only this was no damn game. This was Jo's life. When he turned toward the warehouse, the sound became weaker. Frantically he swung in the opposite direction, and the signal strengthened again. All he could see was scattered trash and an overflowing Dumpster. Murmuring a fervent prayer, he jumped out of the car and rounded the bin. He almost stumbled over a body on the cracked blacktop.

"Jo!" His voice was barely above a whisper as he dropped to his knees beside her. "Oh, God, Jo." She didn't move, didn't respond to his touch. With his heart blocking his windpipe, he gently turned her over. For several seconds his mind refused to process what he was seeing. When it finally started to work again, he shuddered in horror. The front of her blouse was soaked with blood. With shaking fingers, he searched for a pulse at the base of her neck. No matter how hard he pressed or where he shifted his touch, he couldn't find any sign of life. Feeling as if someone had sliced through his own heart, he gathered her tenderly in his arms. His face pressed into her soft red hair; tears stung his eyes. *I love you, Jo. I'll always love you.*

"I'M SAFE. Finally."

The words of awe and relief filled Jo's mind. They didn't reach her lips. In fact, she couldn't feel her mouth forming the syllables. Couldn't feel the air moving in and out of her lungs. Couldn't connect with her body at all. For just a moment, a sense of panic threatened to swamp her. But the fear evaporated almost before it could take any kind of shape.

She didn't need her body. Not here.

Here?

She opened her eyes wider and looked around. At least, that was how her mind perceived what she was doing. But there was nothing to see besides the warm golden glow that enveloped her. She felt herself opening to it, accepting the sense of safety, freedom and well-being that poured over her like healing rays.

She didn't realize she'd put the thoughts into words—or that anyone was there to hear. But an answer came into her mind as if someone standing very close to her had spoken.

"I understand."

She raised her head, felt herself smile. Words weren't necessary. Yet she spoke again. "You're here to greet me."

"Not exactly."

"Then what?"

"You still have work to do on earth."

She had let go of the earth. "No."

"Look in back of you."

She tried to resist, but she felt herself turning. It seemed as if she had traveled an immense distance in time and space. She was amazed to discover that she wasn't far from the place where her body lay on the ground. Or maybe it was a trick of perception that made it seem as if she were hovering only a few dozen feet in the air above a stretch of cracked and bloody pavement.

To her astonishment, she saw herself lying pale and still as death. But that wasn't what drew her attention. Cam was there, leaning over her, pressing his lips to her hair as tears leaked from his eyes.

"Oh, God, Jo!" His voice was rough with grief, tugging at her heart. With a jolt she remembered why she had come down to the warehouse area in the first place.

"He needs me," she murmured.

"Yes."

She felt a rush of urgency. "Will you let me go back to him?"

"It isn't up to me. It could be too late."

"I have to try." She turned and began to fight her way in the direction from which she'd come. At first she met terrible resistance—as if the very atmosphere were trying to hold her in this place where matter and energy met. Returning wasn't an option. She belonged here now. That was why she had left her body and sailed away from the earth like a butterfly swept from a garden by a strong breeze.

It was so tempting to just give up and yield to the inevitable.

But her gaze—all of her attention—was focused on the man who held her body in his arms. She saw his shoulders heave. Heard the despair in his voice. With a burst of inner strength, she galvanized her efforts for one last, wrenching try.

Chapter Two

The wail of an ambulance broke the terrible silence like a mourner's sob at a wake. As if he were coming out of a dream, Cam looked in the direction of the approaching vehicle. He should stand up so the driver could see him, but his limbs felt as if they'd been set in concrete.

Reverently his hands traced the lines of Jo's pale face as if by some miracle his touch could rouse her. Coming to rest at the base of her neck, his fingers sought the point where life once surged.

As he pressed her precious flesh, he felt a weak vibration. Stunned, he went absolutely still, sure that his mind was playing tricks, and he was simply imagining the thing he wanted so much. But it was no illusion. He felt a pulse.

The ambulance had shut off its siren. "Over here! Hurry," Cam yelled before turning his attention back to Jo.

He forgot to breathe as he counted the faint beats and looked at the lighted dial of his watch. He'd been sure she was dead. Now her heartbeat was erratic, but getting stronger, and he felt a surge of hope, as if he'd witnessed a miracle. Moments later, a man and a woman from the rescue squad were kneeling with him on the ground. Knowing there was nothing more he could do, he gave her into their care.

It was agonizing to watch and listen as they worked over her. And startling when he suddenly became aware of her breathing. When had it started?

Straining to hear, he could tell the rhythm was punctuated by a terrible sucking noise. "What's wrong?" he grated.

"Sounds like a pneumothorax—a collapsed lung," the woman said in clipped tones as she ripped open a sealed package and pressed a dressing to the ugly chest wound.

"Will she make it?"

"She's lost a lot of blood." The attendant turned away and started an IV.

"I'm riding with her," Cam said as they shifted her onto a stretcher and lifted it into the van.

"And I'll have your car delivered to the hospital."

He whirled to see Dan Cassidy standing on the cracked pavement. Behind him were three police cars. He'd been so focused on Jo that he hadn't heard anything besides the ambulance pull up in the lot.

"Thanks, Dan, for everything."

"You go on. I'll see you in the waiting room."

The ride to the Maryland Shock Trauma Center was the longest fifteen minutes of Cam's life. His gaze never left Jo's face. His ears strained to hear the heart monitor.

Clutching her hand, he tried to will his strength into her injured body. "Come on, Jo. You're a fighter. Hang on, honey. You can do it. For me. Please. I love you." Over and over he repeated the words, as he prayed the sound of his voice would make a difference to her.

THERE WAS NO CLEAR moment when Jo awoke. First she was vaguely aware of machinery and sounds around her. Cam's lab? No. She was lying in a bed, and tubes were attached to her body, tying her to the earth so she wouldn't drift back into the clouds.

Back into the clouds?

She stumbled over the strangely disturbing thought, tried to catch herself and grasped only confusion. Pain was there, too, but far away, as if some sort of short circuit prevented her from feeling more than gently probing tendrils of discomfort.

"Jo?"

Cam was beside her. Holding her hand. Calling her. He'd been calling her before, hadn't he? Or was that one of her strange dreams? She turned toward him. Tried to squeeze his fingers. But even that small gesture was beyond her capability. Her lids fluttered, and she struggled to keep them open so she could see him.

His fingers tightened around hers. "Jo."

She managed to say his name in return, but that took every bit of her strength.

"Don't talk. Just remember that I love you, need you."

She waited, collected her energy and put forth a tremendous effort. "Wha...happened?" The question was barely a whisper on her lips. But he leaned close so that he could hear.

"You were shot. But you're in the hospital. You're going to be fine."

Was that the hot pain she'd felt in her chest? A bullet? She tried to grab on to the memory. It had been wiped away by the drifting, peaceful time.

She wanted to hang on to consciousness, to hang on to Cam. The effort was too great. Like a boat sinking into deep water, she slowly submerged into blessed sleep.

THE MAN WITH the ruined face bent over the keyboard of his top-of-the-line Pentium computer. Information was power, and he could feel it flowing from his fingertips across the network like a sorcerer sending out a spell. He'd parlayed the buying and selling of data into an international fortune, then lost all but a few million pounds. But he still had his wits, and that would be enough to win his way to the top of the heap again—just the way he had before, by theft and trickery and any means at his disposal.

He raised his hand from the keyboard and touched the rubbery skin on his cheek in a gesture that had become habit when he was alone. Not even the world's most skillful plastic surgeons had been able to restore his face to anything approaching normal. He still looked more like a melted wax candle than a human being.

What had happened to him two years ago would have driven a lesser man insane. But he was made of stiffer stuff. He had the will to hold himself together. And he could live with his face. In fact, he'd found his new appearance useful, now that he was finally getting back to business in earnest. Once, the government and corporate leaders of the world had merely feared his power. Henceforth, they would fear his appearance, as well.

After the fire, when he had awakened in agony, his first thoughts had been focused on revenge. He would stay alive so he could reach out and smite the traitor who had won his trust and then betrayed it.

When he'd been able to think more clearly, he'd taken the longer view. He'd settle up—in good time. And revenge would be all the sweeter because he would not only bring down the bloody traitor, he would destroy everyone who had given him aid and comfort, as well. Starting with Mr. and Mrs. Cameron Randolph. They didn't know it, but they were going to finance his re-entry into the world of high-stakes players.

The man with the nightmare face pounded at the computer keyboard with staccato bursts. Things were coming to a critical point, forcing him to take danger-ous risks if he was going to collect on his investment in Mr. and Mrs. Randolph. But now that he'd finally set his plans into operation, the old feeling of power was like a drug—making him itch to know the outcome of the operation at the warehouse.

Jo WAS NEVER ABLE to remember the first few days in the hospital very clearly. Finally she felt different— stronger, more anchored to the world. In fact, she was anchored by a whole slew of tubes and wires. Opening her eyes, she saw the medical equipment around her bed clearly for the first time.

She also saw her husband sleeping in a chair beside her. God, how long had he been camping out here?

"Cam," she called softly.

He came awake as if someone had fired a cannon next to his chair. When he saw her face, he breathed out a long, shuddering sigh. "Welcome back." Leaning over her, he stroked gentle fingers against her cheek. "Have I told you recently how much I love you?"

"I love you, too," she whispered, closing her eyes and turning her face into his hand. "What happened? How long have I been here?"

"Three days."

"Sheez." She tried without success to push herself up.

"Don't move. Your chest is all bandaged up."

Cautiously she felt the thick layer of gauze and glanced at Cam questioningly. He looked awful—his shirt rumpled, his hair hanging in his face, a dark stubble of beard on his cheeks and chin. He was wearing his glasses instead of his usual contacts, and his gray eyes were bloodshot. Was there a flash of anger in them, too? It was gone before she could be sure.

"Cam? Are you mad about something?"

He shook his head tightly, and she knew that he was lying. But she didn't have the energy to press him.

"What do you remember?" he asked.

Grateful that he'd changed the subject, she switched gears and tried to think about what had happened, but she could grasp only blurry images and the sensation of a hot pain in her chest. "Was I...shot?"

"Yes. And you had a collapsed lung. I thought—" He sucked in a draft of air. "I thought I'd lost you."

"The tunnel," she said dreamily.

His fingers tightened on hers. "What tunnel? The Harbor Tunnel? What route did you take to the warehouse?"

"I—" Jo stopped, her head swimming in confusion as she tried to think about driving. Instead, hazy memories floated through her mind. The bright light. The strange feeling of being out of her body. And a conversation. With someone important. She wasn't sure any of that had happened. And she suddenly felt very spooky.

"Cam—"

His face looked drawn as he stared down at her. "I'm sorry. Forget about answering questions now."

Feeling cold and clammy, she slumped back into the pillows.

A nurse had appeared behind Cam. "She needs to rest, Mr. Randolph," she said kindly but firmly. "You'd be better off going home now and getting some sleep yourself."

"Not while she's still awake."

Jo tried to squeeze Cam's hand, but couldn't muster the strength. Her lids fluttered closed, and the warm darkness claimed her again.

THE NURSE WAS RIGHT. He'd better go home, because he was so close to the edge that he was coming unraveled. He'd almost started demanding answers from Jo when he knew she wasn't in any shape for an interrogation.

He gave her one last kiss and drove back to his cold, empty house—where he lay in bed listening to the sound of the rain pounding on the roof, staring at the exposed beam ceiling. His brain had passed beyond dog tired to a near-zombie state, yet he couldn't fall asleep. Closing his eyes, he turned on his side and automatically reached for Jo's warm body, craving the feel of her soft skin against his naked flesh. His arms encountered nothing but air. Jo wouldn't be back home for almost a week—if she didn't have any setbacks. And he couldn't pull her close even then—not with all those bandages swathing her chest. He drew in a deep breath and let it out slowly. God, he needed to make love to her. More than that, he needed to hear the truth from her.

What was she hiding? What had she been doing at that warehouse that she didn't want him to know?

He couldn't stop his mind from churning. Or stop remembering how it had felt when he'd thought he'd lost the woman he loved. Thank the Lord she was out of danger. Physically. But would things ever be the same between them?

Without warning his mind leapt back to the way his life had been a few years ago when his scientific experiments and inventions had been his biggest source of excitement and satisfaction. Before he'd learned to trust Jo, he'd thought women were more interested in the Randolph fortune than in him. She'd changed his mind and changed his life.

His gaze traveled over the empty side of the bed. He couldn't stay here—wanting her and not even being sure where he stood with her. Getting up, he pulled on sweatpants and a T-shirt. After splashing cold water on his face, he wandered downstairs, past the kitchen to the basement door.

His midnight wanderings took him to the lab. Work was still his salvation when his mind was troubled. And tonight he needed to be in this room.

He powered up the experimental equipment he'd designed for the venture he and Jim Crowley from the Defense Department had dubbed Project Pulsar. He was trying to compress low-level waves—below commercial radio frequencies so that they could carry more civilian and military communications traffic—but so far he wasn't having much success. As he checked his notes and fiddled with the computer settings, he remembered the new approach he'd been mulling over when he'd gotten that mind-shattering call from Jo. Bringing up the editor, he typed in the new algorithm.

At first, he didn't notice any improvement in performance. Damn! Was he ever going to hit on the right combinations of variables? Then the machine beeped, and the readings on the screen doubled, tripled, quadrupled before falling back to where they had been.

Cam's eyes narrowed. What in blazes had caused the surge?

His gaze swept around the lab. No other equipment was turned on. Nobody else was here. Yet he had the sense that he wasn't alone, that someone—something—was watching him intently, anxiously waiting for him to touch the wave compressor again. The hairs on the back of his neck stirred as he looked toward the door and then checked the alarm system. According to the readouts, the house and grounds were secure.

You're losing it, Randolph, he told himself for the second time that evening as he tried to shake off the feeling of eyes drilling into the back of his neck.

Resolutely he turned back to the system and ran the experiment again. This time, contrary to his usual conservative approach, he upped the energy level and squared the output.

The air in the lab crackled like static in a storm. He reached to shut down the power. Before his hand connected with the switch, his muscles froze. A helpless spectator, he watched as a vague shape began to form and shimmer like a desert mirage in the space above his console. Cam rubbed his eyes. When he looked again, the aberration was still there. Incredibly the shades of gray intensified and coalesced. The phenomenon moved away from the bank of machines to the center of the room. To his amazement, it resolved into an almost human form.

What in the name of God was going on? It appeared as if the transport system from *Star Trek* was beaming someone right into his lab, except the person was stuck in limbo between energy and matter. For a second he risked a quick look at the monitor. He'd never seen such extraordinary readings. Neither had he seen anything like what was forming in front of him.

It had glided a few feet closer to him, and he almost turned and sprinted from the lab. But his scientific curiosity won out over fear. Instead of beating a safe retreat, he looked around the room for something that wouldn't conduct electricity. The plastic attachment from his shop vac wasn't a very scientific tool, but it would have to do.

Alert for any sudden change, he moved close to the apparition. It was still out of focus. Tentatively Cam poked the extension wand toward the thing. With a whoosh, he was pulled forward like a piece of dust being sucked into the vacuum.

He dug in his heels and tugged. The air flared with sparkles of color, and the thing tugged back as if it had clamped invisible hands around the end of the wand.

It was fighting him. Was it alive?

Using all his strength, Cam jerked once more and yanked the pole free. Stumbling backward, he caught himself on the edge of a table and stared at the shimmering molecules. His heart hammered as he tried to explain why a door to the twilight zone had opened in his laboratory. It appeared that the man-shaped image was somehow correlated to the Pulsar energy levels. But why had it taken this form? And why was it reacting to *him?* If he didn't know better, he'd swear he'd tuned in a ghost with his equipment. But that was crazy.

Still, he'd better pull the plug on Pulsar until he could get some better monitoring equipment.

Not yet. One more test, the inventor in him countered. Skirting around the specter, he returned to the keyboard and typed in new commands. The molecules of the image began to rotate like tiny pieces of glass in a kaleidoscope. Out of the random patterns, a ragged face emerged at what he supposed was the front of the head.

It remained for only a few seconds. Then, with another loud burst of static, the whole thing vanished back into the ether. Shaken to the bone, Cam stared at the place where it had been, groping for some logical explanation for the most illogical thing he'd ever experienced.

Chapter Three

Jo had never quite gotten used to the luxury of being married to a man like Cameron Randolph or living on an estate, which she'd wryly dubbed the "Plantation." Not when she'd been born and raised in the backwoods of western Maryland where being well-off meant your mom was a waitress at a ski resort and your dad drove a lumber truck. Life with her first husband, private detective Skip O'Malley, had been a lot more comfortable. But it had been a far cry from this.

From where she lay on the chaise longue, Jo looked out over the grounds of the home she and Cam had built near Owings Mills. It was early October, but the flower beds were still lush with all sorts of plants.

She'd taken care of the yard at her old house in Roland Park, and she still liked to do some of the planting and pruning herself. But now it was a hobby, not a necessity, since a garden service came in twice a week to keep the estate in perfect order. They'd already been here for a couple of hours this morning.

In the distance she could see Monroe, the head gardener, mulching the beds around the pool. A few minutes later, on his way to his pickup, he paused at the edge of the patio. "I'll have those ornamental cabbages you asked for by next week, Mrs. Randolph."

"That's fine. I like your new beds around the pools and patio."

He smiled briefly. "Thank you, ma'am."

Jo watched Monroe push the wheelbarrow up the path. Having help for the heavy outside work was one thing. But when Cam had asked if she wanted a full-time staff to take care of the house, she'd refused. Servants underfoot all the time would have made her feel weird, so she convinced her husband she could "make do" with a cleaning woman who came in three times a week. Until this morning, there had also been a practical nurse on duty twenty-four hours a day. Jo hadn't protested, since recovering from a major chest wound was no Sunday-school picnic. Besides, it was the only way Cam would leave her and go in to the office. Still, it was a relief to finally have the woman out of her hair.

She closed her eyes and tried to will some of the frazzled feeling from her body. She and Cam hadn't really been alone in days. And the strain was getting to her, although that wasn't the only thing causing a rift between them.

She'd made a bad decision. She knew that now. It was a mistake not to have told him about her investigation. Of course, when she confessed what she'd been doing down at the warehouse, he was going to be furious. But anger was insignificant compared to the danger of losing his trust.

A buzzer sounded. Someone was at the gate. Jo pushed herself painfully off the chaise and made her way toward the house.

"I'm coming," she called, although whoever was leaning on the bell couldn't hear her until she pushed the intercom button. It and the locked gate were part of the elaborate security system that Cam installed when they'd moved in. She hated the precautions, but she'd agreed to go along with them. After all, her husband did have millions of dollars' worth of high-tech equipment in his home lab.

"Yes?"

A deliveryman's face and shoulders appeared on the television screen in the alcove by the front door. "Flowers for Mrs. Randolph."

"From whom?"

"Mr. Randolph."

Jo smiled. Well, that was thoughtful of him. "I'll buzz you through." She pressed the button that opened the gate. A minute later, a familiar green-and-yellow Lancaster's truck pulled up in front of the portico, and the deliveryman got out.

The arrangement he brought to the door was beautiful—a dozen red roses with sprays of baby's breath in a silver bowl.

Jo gave the man a generous tip and took the flowers into the family room where she could look at them while she rested on the couch.

Tucked into one side was a white envelope.

Smiling again, she drew out the rectangular card. But the smile froze as she read the words.

Nothing has changed, Mrs. Randolph. If you go to the police or tell your husband about your confidential investigation, I can snuff him out as easily as I arranged to deliver these blossoms to you.

Aghast, she stared from the note to the arrangement and back again. By the time she finished reading it for the second time, her breath was coming in ragged little gasps. Her fingers closed around the card, squeezing it into misshapen pleats that dug into her flesh.

Sickness rose in her throat and, dizzy, she sank down onto the sofa and cradled her head in her hands. God, what was she going to do now?

She almost jumped up and called Cam. Or Dan Cassidy. But a terrible feeling of being watched stopped her. Her scalp crawled as she looked around. It was almost as if someone was in the house with her, waiting to see what she'd do. All at once she realized when she'd felt this way before. Three years ago when a psychotic killer named Art Nugent had been stalking her, invading her house, setting deadly traps.

Who was it this time? she thought. The deliveryman? Was he still here? Swaying on her feet, she went back to the security system monitor and did a status check. The display showed that the vehicle had cleared the gate at 1120 hours. And the estate was closed up tight again. Only the gardener was somewhere on the grounds. She could picture him trying to defend her with a rake and a hoe, and it was all she could do to hold back a hysterical laugh. Several minutes passed before she was thinking straight enough to take the next logical step.

In the yellow pages she found the ad for the florist and dialed the number from the kitchen phone.

A pleasant-sounding woman answered. "Lancaster's. May I help you?"

"I just received some flowers from my husband."

"Is there some problem with them?"

"No. I—I just wanted to check and see when they were sent."

"Certainly. Can I have your name?"

"Jo O'Malley. My husband is Cameron Randolph."

"One moment, please."

The woman was gone for much longer than Jo expected. When she came back on the line, her voice was apologetic. "Mrs. Randolph—uh, Ms. O'Malley—we have no record of an order from your husband today. Perhaps the delivery came from another florist."

"Yes, I guess I must have made a mistake," Jo managed to say, and hung up the receiver. But she knew she hadn't gotten it wrong. The driver had been from Lancaster's. And the truck. She recognized it because Cam always used that company.

Had someone snuck the bogus order onto the van after the vehicle left the shop? Or were the man and his truck an elaborate fake?

Feeling trapped and unable to cope, she leaned heavily on the kitchen counter. After a minute, she pushed herself up, dashed into the family room and snatched up the flowers, holding them at arm's length. She was about to throw them in the trash when she stopped herself.

She didn't want the hateful things in the house, but they were important evidence. On shaky legs, she carried the arrangement to the laundry room and shoved it in the cabinet above the washer.

Lord, what should she do? As a private investigator, she'd advised so many people who were in trouble, and they always saw her as a tower of strength. But now that she was smack in the middle of this mess, she couldn't think straight.

The only thing she knew was that it was more important than ever to continue the investigation that had brought her to south Baltimore. But she couldn't do that, either. Not until she got her strength back. Yet there was an alternative—Mike Lancer, a detective who'd worked with her on a number of cases. He was good. And he was discreet. She could ask him to come in on this until she was in shape to take over again. He'd find out what had happened at the florist. And he could try to locate Cam's car. But how much should she tell him about the case?

Slowly, fighting the ache in her chest, she made her way to the den that she'd outfitted as a home office and sat down at her computer.

After booting up the machine, she accessed a private file that she'd been keeping for the past few months. It was protected by a password—which she knew wouldn't lock out a computer wizard like Cam if he was determined to gain access. The best she could hope for was that he'd assume she was maintaining confidential records on clients and respect her privacy.

The hard drive whirred and served up a dossier titled R. E. Investigation. As always, Jo felt a painful knot form in her stomach as she read the first entries. They were a series of typed notes she'd scanned onto her system and then locked in one of her desk drawers down at 43 Light Street.

The first one had arrived in July. Two and a half months ago.

July 20
Dear Ms. O'Malley,
I'm writing to warn you of some potential problems. I can't tell you much yet, but I will know more in the future. However, do not discuss this note with anyone else, including your husband, Cameron Randolph. If you break my confidence you could put his life in serious jeopardy.

                                        A friend

The note had come with the regular mail delivery to her detective agency; the downtown Baltimore postmark hadn't given her any clues to its origins, and there was no return address. In retrospect, she could see that it was far less threatening than the one that had come today with the flowers. Her first impulse had been to dismiss it as the work of a crank and ask Cam if he knew who was out to cause him grief. But fear for his safety had kept her mute. What harm could a quiet investigation of his company do, she'd asked herself. She'd share her findings with Cam as soon as there was anything substantial to tell. But she'd turned up nothing and had almost convinced herself that the note was a vicious prank.

Ten days later she'd gotten another letter—this one, slipped under her office door during the night. In it was a list of Randolph products scheduled for overseas delivery with an asterisk beside several of the consignments. According to her informant, these goods were not going to reach their intended destinations. Further information on who was diverting the shipment would follow. Again, the information was accompanied by a warning not to jeopardize Cam's life by discussing what she'd learned.

A week after that Jo had received the note that had sent her to the warehouse area on Saturday afternoon with her camera to get some hard evidence.

Appended to it was a sketchy account she'd tried to type yesterday of the incident that had put her in the hospital. She'd wanted to write more, but she'd found to her disgust that the attack was almost totally wiped from her memory. Maybe it was her mind's way of protecting itself. Still, some pretty terrible things had happened in her life, and she remembered *them*. She closed her eyes and struggled once more to bring the scene into focus.

After several minutes, she realized with a sick feeling that Cam had come home without her knowing it and was standing behind her, his gray eyes boring into the computer monitor.

White faced, she whirled around in her chair.

The space in back of her was as empty of humanity as a mirror in a vacant room.

"Cam?"

No one answered.

"Cam? Quit playing hide-and-seek." She heard the high, strangled sound of her voice.

No one was there. Yet she felt as if a ghostly figure were standing only a few feet away, watching her with piercing eyes.

Cold sweat broke out on her brow. She might have gotten up and run, but some force seemed to keep her in the desk chair as if strong, unseen hands were pressing on her shoulders. "Don't hurt me," she whispered.

He didn't respond. He? Somehow she knew it was a man. That insight was followed by another. *He* was the one she'd felt watching her when she'd been sitting in the family room with the flowers.

"Who are you?"

He didn't answer, and she felt as if she had a screw loose talking to empty air. But she knew she wasn't wrong.

"Who are you?" she repeated.

Still, silence met the question.

For several seconds she was frozen in place. Then she got up and walked away on shaky legs, wondering if he was going to snake out invisible arms and grab her.

"ARE YOU FEELING okay?"

Jo looked up at Katie Martin and gave her a half smile, wishing fervently that her friends had picked a different day for a visit.

In fact, she'd forgotten all about the group coming over for a late lunch until the buzzer on the gate had sounded again, making her jump like a possum hit with a BB gun.

She couldn't tell anyone why she was in such bad shape, so she'd let them think she was still too tired to be much of a hostess.

"I'm fine," she answered Katie. "It's just frustrating to get bushed so easily."

Noel Zacharias, Sabrina Barkley, Erin Stone, Marissa Devereaux and some of the other women from 43 Light Street had pulled up chairs around the glass-topped patio table.

While they chatted and ate the potluck lunch they'd brought, Jo tried to seem glad of the company. In a way, she was—she didn't want to be alone.

"As soon as you're better, you and Cam need to get away," Marissa said brightly. "Why don't you let Adventures in Travel plan a couple of dream itineraries for you. Greece is wonderful this time of year. Or do the two of you like to cruise? You might enjoy the western Caribbean."

"Well, you've sold *me*," Noel teased.

"I'll have to check with Cam," Jo said, wondering if he'd go, wondering if that was a good way to keep him out of danger.

Katie stood. "It's been wonderful visiting you. But I think we're beginning to wear you out."

"I've enjoyed the company, but I *am* starting to fade," Jo murmured with relief.

Everyone except Noel left the patio. She and Jo had been seeing a lot of each other since Cam and Noel's husband, Jason, had become partners in Randolph Security.

"Are you going to tell me what's wrong?" Noel asked.

"I've been through a pretty grueling ordeal."

"I know you, Jo. You're not just recovering from a gunshot wound. You're seriously depressed. I kept watching you while we were laughing and talking. Everybody was having a good time except you."

Jo looked away. She couldn't tell her friend about the flowers—or the ghostly presence that had been reading over her shoulder. But maybe it would help to let some of her feelings out. "You remember when you were in danger, and Jason couldn't tell you the truth about what was going on?"

Noel instantly came to the wrong conclusion. "Do you think Cam's lying to you about something?"

"No. That's not what I meant."

"What did you mean?" a male voice came from the doorway, and Jo jerked toward the sound.

Cam was standing with his hands clenched at his sides.

She stared at him with a mixture of relief and wariness. Until that moment she hadn't realized she was worrying that he wouldn't make it home that evening. She started to run to him. In the next moment, she wondered what would have happened if she'd said something more to Noel—and he'd heard.

"What are you doing, eavesdropping?" she asked. Immediately she wished she'd let her brain catch up with her mouth.

"I wasn't planning it. I live here. I came home to say hello to your friends, and I found the two of you discussing me."

Jo clasped her hands tightly in her lap, afraid that if she let go she'd fall apart.

Noel's cheeks were red, but she lifted her chin and answered the question for Jo. "She didn't start the conversation. I could see something's wrong, and in my heavy-handed way I was trying to find out what's bothering her. So this conversation is my fault, and I'm really sorry I caused any trouble between the two of you." She shot Jo an apologetic look before making a hasty exit.

Jo and Cam were left staring at each other.

Cam felt despair hanging in the air between them like the final notes of a tragic opera. He was standing only fifteen feet away from Jo, yet he had the frightening sensation that the distance was much greater and that if he didn't go to his wife immediately she would slip still further from his reach. But he didn't know how to close the chasm that had been growing wider between them for days.

"Cam." She pushed herself too quickly out of her chair.

Her little wince of pain released him. He met her in the middle of the terrace, reached for her and dropped his arm back to his side in frustration.

He wanted everything to be sure and certain between them—the way it had been on the day they'd said their marriage vows. But right now he'd settle for a lot less. He'd settle for sweeping her into his embrace and making her acknowledge that she wanted him as much as he wanted her. But he couldn't. Instead, he watched her eyes. Today they were picking up color from the baggy jade green shirt she wore. Those blue-green eyes had always been one of the things that he found so intriguing about her. Lately he'd cursed the way they shifted away from him.

Jo was the one who closed the final distance between them, moving toward him slowly with tiny steps—each one tearing at his heart. Delicately she laid her head against his shoulder.

"I love you," she whispered. "I need you. It's terrible feeling like . . . like I can't reach you." The words came out in a fervent rush that made his insides melt.

"Oh, Jo." Closing his eyes, he breathed in her familiar scent. Then his hands sifted through her hair and stroked down her arms. The contact sent little shivers through her body—and through his.

"I'm sorry," they said at the same time.

And then, "It's all right."

He felt her suck in as deep a breath as she could manage. She let it out very slowly and buried her face more deeply against his shoulder. When she shuddered, he imagined some terrible secret bottled up inside her, straining to break free. "What is it?"

"I'm glad you're home."

He waited for something more.

But she didn't speak, and he continued to stroke through her marvelous hair, wondering how he could get the response he needed from her without coming out and begging.

"I can't stand the thought of almost losing you," he finally said.

Silently she inched a little closer to him, held him a little tighter.

"You know I like being in control over my life. Can you imagine what it was like driving up that street and finding you lying on the ground? When I ran toward you, I could see the wind moving your hair, and I kept telling myself that meant you were alive, even though the notion was nonsense."

"Oh, Cam, it must have been awful."

"Then there were the first few minutes when I was holding you but couldn't feel your heartbeat. Everything around me went black, like the light of the sun had been swallowed up."

"I didn't know. I didn't know how bad it was for you."

"Tell me what you're hiding."

"Nothing." She tipped her face up to his, reaching for his lips. A long shuddering sigh went through him as he closed the contact. Gently, gently, he brushed his mouth against hers, needing more but holding himself ruthlessly in check.

"Oh, Cam, it's been so long." She sighed.

That sigh was his undoing. He deepened the kiss, but only as much as he dared, afraid to unleash the hunger that had built relentlessly inside him since he'd brought her home from the hospital. Yet his breath quickened and his body tautened. So did hers.

"You taste so good," he growled, his mouth devouring, his head angling so that he could drink in more of her.

"Cam, I need this. I need *you*," she whispered as she started to undo the buttons of his shirt with shaky hands. When she slipped inside and ran her fingers through the hair on his chest, he felt a shiver of anticipation go through her frame. She wanted him. At least he knew that much. Without conscious thought, he began to move his hips back and forth against hers in the old, familiar rhythm.

He was hard, ready for her, and he wanted her to feel the same urgency to mate with him—to reaffirm their marriage bonds.

He'd learned exactly what she liked, exactly what excited her. His hands stroked lightly but tantalizingly up and down her arms, over her back, under her loose-fitting shirt, making her moan with pleasure.

"Oh, yes. Cam, please."

His palm slid over her right breast—and she gasped.

He went very still. "Jo, I didn't mean to hurt you."

"Don't stop."

He drew in a shuddering breath. "We have to. We can't. *You* can't." He pressed his cheek against the top of her head and fought to get control of his body.

"I shouldn't have started anything," she whispered. "But when I kissed you, I couldn't help it."

"Sweetheart, it takes two to tango."

"But it's worse for you. You're in perfect physical shape. I'm still a wreck."

He laughed. "A red-hot wreck."

She gave him a crooked little smile, but the shadow was back in her blue-green eyes.

He wanted to take her by the shoulders and shake her, make her tell him what secret was bottled up inside her. Instead he stroked his finger on her cheek. "You shouldn't even be standing up this long. We'd better go inside."

He ushered her toward the house. As she stepped across the threshold of the French doors, she stopped suddenly and grasped his arm.

"What's wrong?"

"I felt a hand brush the back of my neck."

"What?"

She shook her head slowly, uncertainly. "That's what it felt like. Cam, if this house were old, I'd swear it was haunted."

"We had it built."

"I know. But do you suppose—" she hesitated and then rushed on "—someone could have died on the property, and they're hanging around trying to communicate with us?"

"That's—"

"Nonsense," she finished for him, then asked quickly, "You haven't noticed anything out of the ordinary, have you?"

"Maybe," he said hesitantly.

"What?"

"In the lab. I had an anomalous matter-energy transfer."

"A what?"

"A phenomenon I couldn't explain with my equipment."

"Are you going to put that in terms I can understand?"

He debated how much to tell her. The next time he'd activated the system, he'd tested it every which way to Christmas. The phenomenon had not been repeated. "I thought I saw an energy field detach itself from the equipment. But it was the night I left you in the hospital," he rushed on. "And I was so strung out, I could have been hallucinating, for all I know."

"Cam—"

"First thing tomorrow I'll have Dan Aykroyd and the *Ghostbusters* crew out here to sweep the place," he said with forced heartiness.

She looked as if she were as eager to drop the subject as he, yet she went on. "There *is* one other possibility... What if the ghost is connected to one of us?"

"What do you mean?" he asked.

"Someone who died. Like your brother, or my husband, Skip—but he wouldn't do this to us."

He'd do it to me, Cam thought. *Skip O'Malley and I always did hate each other's guts.* Then he backed off. The idea of being haunted by a ghost—from his past or any other place—was too far out to reconcile with his scientific training.

Jo still looked troubled. "Remember before we were married when that psycho Art Nugent was after me? He was going to kill me. You don't think he could come back from the grave to get me, do you?"

"Of course not." He gave her a direct look. "Maybe we're conjuring up weird experiences because it's easier than facing what's wrong between us," he suggested tightly, watching her face.

She looked startled.

"I'll go first." He found himself blurting one of the things that had been on his mind since he'd sat beside her hospital bed staring at her bloodless face. "I want you to quit being a private detective."

She blinked. "Did I hear you right?"

"Detective work is too dangerous for a married woman. And you take too damn many chances."

"I don't take chances." She turned away from him and sat on the couch.

"Oh, yeah. Then why in the hell were you down at that warehouse by yourself? Who were you working for on that case?"

The blood drained from her face. "That's... that's confidential information."

"Who am I going to tell?"

"Cam, please. I understand how you feel, but don't press me on this."

He took her advice, because he suspected he wasn't ready for the answer. What the hell did you do when the wife you'd always trusted started lying to you? And not even a direct question could pry the truth out of her.

"What would I do if I gave up my career?" she suddenly asked.

The rejoinder had been rhetorical, but he had an answer ready. In a way, it was a test he'd been devising in his mind since he'd decided Jo wasn't being straight with him. Maybe he was all wrong and she *was* working for some mysterious client who'd demanded absolute confidentiality. But if she really loved him, she'd prove it. "Stay home and take care of our children."

"Children?"

"Yeah, as in babies. Raise a family."

"But... but we've never talked about having children."

"I know. We've *both* been too wrapped up in our careers. But while I was waiting to find out if you were going to live or die, I kept thinking that if I lost you, I'd have nothing of you left. Nothing."

She raised her eyes pleadingly to his. "Oh, Cam, I don't know how... how to cope with this."

"You're good at coping. Or you will be when you get your strength back."

"I don't think I'd be a very good mother," she blurted.

"You'd be great."

"I didn't exactly have a peachy childhood. Remember, my mother was too busy scraping a living to have much energy left over for her kids. We sort of raised ourselves and—"

"And you turned out just fine. Besides, the situation is completely different. We're not scraping along. We've got plenty of money. You can have all the help you need. And while you're home, you'll have time to work on that detective novel you've always wanted to write. You can have a whole new career."

"You mean, I hole up in my office while a nanny raises the children?"

He looked exasperated. "I didn't mean it that way, and you know it. I was trying to point out the advantages of changing your life-style."

"I don't know what to say."

"Think about it."

He couldn't take the stricken look on her face, so he got up and gestured toward the library where they'd set up a hospital bed so she wouldn't have to climb the stairs. "You'd better go get some rest." Without waiting for a reply, he turned and left her sitting alone on the couch.

Chapter Four

Cam picked up the extension in the lab on the second ring.

"Got a minute?" Jason Zacharias asked.

"Yes. What have you found out?" The night after his inconclusive talk with Jo, Cam had decided he couldn't live with uncertainty. If his wife didn't trust him, he'd have to find out what was going on with his own resources. Even if the information tore out his heart. So he'd asked for Jason's help. As vice president of Randolph Security and one of Cam's best friends, Jason was the only person he trusted to check up on Jo. Still, it made them both uncomfortable.

There was a long pause that Cam didn't much like. "Let's start with the car," Jason finally said.

"You've found it?"

"No. And neither have the police in a fifteen-state area. It hasn't surfaced at any legitimate outlets. And it hasn't been spotted at any of those fly-by-night auction sales, either. We're still checking out-of-state outlets and the chop shops."

"I can't believe it was a random car jacking. They were after my computer equipment."

"Or the data you've got stored in it. Are you using the voice-activated feature to make notes on Pulsar while you're driving?" Jason asked.

"Yeah. But nobody knows about Pulsar."

Jason didn't answer, and Cam filled the silence with a mirthless laugh. "I almost hope the sons of bitches go after the computer. I'd love to be there to see the looks on their faces when they try to get it out of the car."

"Sure, the way you've wired it, the thing will blow the minute they touch it with a screwdriver." Jason snorted. Then his voice sobered. "You really don't want them to destroy a million dollars' worth of equipment."

"Not if I have a choice." Cam picked up the metal Chinese exercise balls on his desk and rotated them with his fingers. They were supposed to relieve stress. Today their jangly little sound made him edgy. "What about the warehouse?" he finally asked.

"R. L. Simms and Sons holds the lease on the place."

"That name sounds familiar."

There was another awkward hiatus. "It should. They're the new shipping company your orders department signed with last year."

"And?" Cam prompted.

"Over half the inventory in the place is Randolph Electronics equipment." Jason sounded as unhappy about delivering the news as Cam was to hear it.

"Oh, hell."

"That may not mean anything," his friend hurried to add. "There was merchandise from other local companies, too."

"I want a complete check on Simms and Sons and anybody else they're doing business with."

"I'll get right on it," Jason promised. "The Simms connection probably doesn't have anything to do with the car jacking. They're not in the greatest neighborhood, and it's practically deserted on Saturdays.''

"I know," he agreed. Yet he wasn't willing to make any assumptions until he had all the facts. He cleared his throat. "And what about the other stuff I asked you to check on, like the previous history of the Plantation?"

"I've researched the deeds and correlated them with local newspaper accounts. I can't find any record of violence connected with the land.''

"But?" Cam picked up on his friend's tone of voice again.

"Someone else has been checking the records.''

"Are you sure?''

"Yes, the clerk at the county courthouse commented.''

"Did she say who it was?''

"No, but I'll find out.''

WHILE CAM TALKED to Jason, Jo stood in the bathroom, a short terry robe tied loosely around her naked body.

She glanced at the V where the robe overlapped in front. The bandages had been gone for almost a week. That was something positive. And in the hospital, she'd dropped ten pounds. So her hips were fashionably thin. Too bad she'd never been concerned with fashion.

On the other hand, she had always taken her normal body image for granted. Which was why she felt a little shock of disbelief every time she saw the angry red surgical scar that made it look as if someone had tried to carve her up for Thanksgiving dinner.

Still, that wasn't the worst. Jo sucked in a steadying breath and slid her gaze upward from the scar to her right breast where the bullet had pierced her body. Along the inside curve, the wound was still puckered and indented. She turned from side to side, inspecting the knitted flesh from several angles.

She'd seen Cam wince when he saw it. What about when he touched it? She squeezed her eyes shut. Maybe that wasn't going to be a problem. Cam hadn't made a move toward her since the afternoon he'd overheard her conversation with Noel. And it wasn't simply because he was afraid of hurting her.

All she had to do was go downstairs and tell her husband why she'd been at the warehouse—and he'd stop acting as though there were a glass wall between them. But she couldn't risk it. Not until she had the straight scoop.

Mike had called her back the day after the flower incident. Unfortunately his report hadn't amounted to a hill of beans. The driver was the regular guy from Lancaster's, all right. He'd found the flowers in the back of the truck and assumed someone had left the delivery off the sheet. So he'd decided the best thing to do was bring them out here. He couldn't tell Mike any more than that.

Jo pressed her knuckles against her mouth. Maybe she and Cam couldn't talk, but there *was* something she could do to repair their marriage.

Stepping out of the bathroom, Jo crossed to the spacious walk-in closet. The granny gown she'd been wearing for the past few nights was hanging on a hook by the door. Bypassing it, she opened the drawer where she kept the sexy nighties she'd gotten since marrying Cam.

As she stroked her fingertips over the silky fabric, she felt the familiar tingle of excitement in the pit of her

stomach. When she started looking at the gowns, however, her spirits plummeted again. Most were cut low in
front, so that the ugly red scar on her breast would be
the first thing Cam saw. Searching through the drawer,
she found there was one with a lace yoke that managed
to be both demure and provocative.

After slipping it over her head, Jo turned toward the
full-length mirror. The scar was hidden by the placket
of tiny buttons down the front, but delicate hints of her
curves were revealed by the translucent fabric. Yes, it
ought to do very nicely.

Before she could start for the lab, however, more
doubts assailed her. What about her other big problem? Cam had practically blown her away when he'd
asked her to give up the detective agency and start a
family.

She sighed. They hadn't talked about it since he'd
dropped his bombshell. But she'd been playing the
conversation over and over in her mind. Getting preg-
nant was a big step. Certainly it would be a mistake if
you were only doing it to make your husband happy—
particularly if he hadn't really thought the whole thing
through. But then on the other hand, what if he turned
it into such a loaded issue that it destroyed your marriage?

Jo felt a pulse begin to pound in her throat. Was the
unresolved question going to come between them when
he saw her? Would it spoil their lovemaking? Or keep
anything from getting started? Before she lost her nerve
she crossed to her bedside table, got out her diaphragm
and took it into the bathroom. Then she hurried downstairs.

But as she padded barefoot across the first-floor hall,
she was struck again by the eerie sensation of being

watched that kept overtaking her at unpredictable moments. Cam had joked about having the Ghostbusters sweep the house. She wished a service like that really did exist so she'd know for sure what was going on.

Halting in her tracks, she felt a steady gaze burning into her back.

"You!" She whirled around and peered down the hall.

It was as empty as a moonlit field. Yet she *knew* a ghostly presence was hovering in the shadows.

"What do you want?" she called, hating the quaver in her voice. The ghost didn't answer.

"Please stop playing with me," she pleaded.

Was she imagining a subtle change in the quality of the silence around her? As if the ghost was sorry he'd frightened her? Could it really be someone she knew— her mother, her father, Skip? Then she thought again about Art Nugent, the man who had stalked her, and the possessive way he'd insisted on getting close to her before he'd kidnapped her and taken her to his house. It was like that now. Only more intense, if that were possible.

"Leave me alone!" she said aloud and hurried toward the door to the spacious lower level.

The admonition seemed to have an effect. Or maybe it was just that as she descended the steps to the lab, she put the ghost firmly out of her mind and focused all her attention on her husband. Probably most of their friends hadn't given the marriage between an introverted scientist with a Ph.D. in physics and a sassy detective who'd only completed high school much of a chance, but she and Cam had made it work—until recently. She bit back a sigh of distress. Under normal circumstances she didn't mind that he'd stay down here past midnight when a new idea absorbed his interest. Giving each other space had been an important part of the relationship. But lately, she knew he was deliberately disappearing down to the lab to avoid her.

Her mouth dry as cotton, she stopped abruptly in the doorway and watched him. He was wearing a white lab coat and bending over some equipment, adjusting dials. Every so often he glanced from the controls to a large CRT monitor in the corner of the room. It flickered with a weird intensity that made her eyes hurt, and she looked away.

Cam turned from the screen to his readouts. An adjustment didn't seem to affect the phenomenon. While she watched the play of muscles in his back, he stiffened as if he knew he was being observed. For several seconds he stood absolutely still. Then he turned toward the door. The wary expression on his face lessened a little when he saw her.

Jo managed a wispy greeting. "Hi."

"Hi," he replied cautiously.

"Were you expecting someone else?"

"No," he said too quickly. "I thought you were going to bed."

She stepped out of the shadows and into the spot where she knew the light would show the curves of her body through her silky gown. "Not yet."

He shifted his weight from one foot to the other, and she felt his gaze on her, hot and wanting. Still she sensed his resistance.

"Cam." She swayed toward him, totally caught up in her response to this man that she loved so much.

"You shouldn't have come down here."

"You're wrong." She glided across the floor, her eyes boldly holding his but her heart thumping so fast and hard that she could barely breathe.

"Jo. I don't want—"

"I think you do." She raised up on tiptoes, intent on stopping the conversation in the most effective way possible. But it was Cam who closed the distance, lowering his mouth to hers with a primitive growl that robbed her of breath. Weeks of frustration fired the kiss. He claimed her mouth with savage possessiveness, his lips opening hers so that he could ravage her hungrily. She welcomed the assault.

Deep down, she'd been afraid that he wouldn't let her get this close. Now joy surged through her, and her arms wound around his neck, pulling him closer.

He shifted his grip, his hands sliding down her body to cup her bottom and pull her hips against his. When she gasped, he drew back, and his arms dropped away from her.

A surge of light in the corner of the room caught the edge of her vision. The screen behind Cam was going wild, as if it understood what was happening and was somehow responding to the powerful emotions—positive and negative—the two of them were generating.

"I hurt you again," Cam said, sighing.

"No. I won't break." The flickering brilliance behind Cam was eclipsed by the mixture of wanting and regret that had turned his gray eyes to charcoal. She took his face in her palms, stroking the dark stubble of beard that she'd always found so sexy. "The only thing that hurts is needing to make love to you so badly that I can't stand it."

He stared down at her as if he still couldn't quite believe the invitation.

''Please.'' She held her breath, waiting, wanting.

Lifting his trembling hands, he let out a shuddering breath as he cradled her breasts, his fingertips cresting over her hardened nipples. Wobbly on her feet, she reached to steady herself against his broad shoulders. When he intensified the touch, the pleasure was so sharp that she cried out once more.

''Oh, Cam. Oh, Cam,'' she breathed, white-hot desire building so quickly inside her that she felt as if she might burst into flames.

There was no question of trying to make it upstairs to the bedroom. It was much too far away.

''The office.''

''Yes.''

Together they stumbled toward the comfortably furnished work area off the main lab. It had a wonderful fleece rug that they'd taken advantage of on a number of occasions.

Jo was in front of Cam. As they reached the office doorway she heard him gasp, surprise and pain mingling in his voice.

Whirling, she saw his face contort as he grabbed the doorframe to keep from sinking to the floor.

''What's wrong?'' she questioned urgently.

He didn't answer, but behind him the screen that had drawn her attention earlier pulsed with unholy light, as if it were possessed by a demon. Yet it wasn't just the monitor. Some kind of strange energy field had taken over half the room. It expanded and contracted, dancing in the air, shimmering and blazing like a laser show they'd seen at the science museum. Transfixed, Jo was unable to turn away. With each pulse of light, she felt a surge of anger.

She tried to grab Cam and drag him through the doorway. But some invisible force kept her from raising her arms, as if the phenomenon in the room had a supernatural hold over her.

Before her eyes, a ball of rippling energy coalesced out of the chaos. For a frightening moment she was sure she saw the distorted features of a man wavering in the air.

"The ghost," she gasped. Then the image blurred, and the shape changed and straightened into an arrow of flame.

As Jo watched in helpless horror, it launched itself at Cam's back.

Chapter Five

The arrow released Jo from her trance, but she couldn't react fast enough. The energy bolt struck Cam in the back. With a strangled cry, he sagged to his knees and toppled forward.

Taking hold of his shirt, Jo tugged with all her strength. The strain sent a sharp pang stabbing through her recent scars. Gritting her teeth, she dragged Cam across the threshold and into the office. Behind her she could see the poltergeist, or whatever it was, glowing and shimmering as if it were collecting itself for another attack. With a moan of fear, she slammed the door and pressed her trembling shoulders against it. The barrier shook and rattled.

"Stop it! Leave him alone," Jo screamed, hardly aware of what she was saying or who she was addressing. But almost at once, the terrible assault stopped.

The sudden silence was deafening. All Jo could hear was blood pounding in her ears as she leapt toward her husband. He lay without moving, his skin the color of ash. Frightened, she pressed her hand against his chest. His heart was beating, but he didn't seem to be breathing.

Fear clawed at her insides, but she couldn't allow herself to fall apart. She took a deep breath and started to give him mouth-to-mouth resuscitation, doing it carefully and methodically.

One, two, three times she forced air into his lungs, then gently depressed his chest to exhale. *You're going to be all right. You have to be all right,* she chanted silently as she kept on with the drill, ignoring the increasing agony in her own chest. As she worked she had a better appreciation of what he must have gone through when he found her shot and lifeless. Her gaze flicked to the telephone. She needed help. But she was afraid to stop the CPR for even a moment.

On the tenth cycle, Cam's own lungs took up the process, and he started to wheeze. He took a gasping breath. Then another and another.

"Thank God." Jo pressed her lips to his temple and grabbed his hand, clasping his flesh with grateful little squeezes.

He stirred, and her gaze riveted to his face. A moment later his eyes opened, and he looked around like a man who'd awakened in a strange room and didn't remember how he'd got there.

"Lie still," she murmured.

Cam's free hand combed through the shaggy fibers of the rug. "What the hell am I doing laid out in my office like a body at a wake?"

"You had an accident." Jo stopped, unsure of how to explain.

Tentatively he touched his chest. "Did I have a heart attack or something?"

"No."

"There was a pain like a red-hot poker shooting through my back and into my lungs." He winced.

"Then a second one. Worse than the first." He made a stab at another explanation. "I guess they couldn't have been bullets. Or I'd be dead."

"Not bullets."

"Then what in blazes?" He turned his head and looked toward the closed door to the lab, his eyes narrowing. "There was something out there. Something alive—but not flesh and blood."

Jo shivered at the description. "Yes. I—I'm not sure what it was. Your CRT was going crazy." Even as she struggled to understand what she'd witnessed, she couldn't help doubting her own senses. "There was some kind of energy flickering all over the whole room. I saw a face. I thought it was the ghost. It contracted into a ball, and the ball turned into an arrow that attacked you."

As she spoke, Jo watched Cam anxiously, but the off-the-wall explanation didn't seem to startle him.

"Just before I looked up and saw you in the doorway, I was getting strange readings on the system again." He cursed vehemently and tried to push himself up.

"Don't. We should call an ambulance."

"I don't need an ambulance. I'm fine."

Her fingers tightened around his hand. "Cam, you stopped breathing. You belong in the emergency room, not in your office."

His eyes locked with hers. "I stopped breathing, and you resuscitated me."

"Yes."

"After you dragged me in here and slammed the door."

She nodded gravely.

His hand came up to gently touch her chest. "You were in no condition for that."

"I did what I had to do."

He shifted his hand so that he could clasp hers. She came down beside him on the rug, snuggling close, and he turned so that he could cradle her gently against his body. They clung to each other like survivors of a natural disaster who had each assumed the other was dead.

"I guess I got a taste of how you've been feeling for the past few weeks," Jo finally whispered.

"God, sweetheart, I'm sorry."

"It wasn't your fault."

His lips stroked along the edge of her cheek, and she closed her eyes, wishing she could shut out everything else but him. This time she didn't protest as Cam carefully pushed himself to a sitting position. She only watched him closely. His color was still a little chalky, but he seemed remarkably well for a man who'd stopped breathing less than half an hour ago.

Her mind scrambled to make sense of what had happened. "Cam, I want to know what's going on. What kind of experiments have you been doing?"

"Some research for the Defense Department."

Her eyes drilled into the closed door as if the room beyond had filled with deadly radiation. "Something dangerous?"

"Of course not! I wouldn't do something dangerous in the same house with you. It's a project to compress low-level energy waves."

She looked at him blankly.

"You know how radio stations and other broadcast media operate on different frequencies—how transmissions can interfere with one another if the frequencies are too close? Well, I'm trying to widen the usable spectrum so more stations can operate at frequencies we couldn't use before. Not for commercial broadcasting, but for personal communications.''

''Why are you working with the DOD? I thought you didn't like bureaucratic red tape.''

''I don't. A guy named Jim Crowley came to me with an offer I couldn't refuse, because he thought I might have the right skills to make some progress in the field. The energy compression premise sounded interesting, so we negotiated a research contract. Nothing big. It's under a million dollars.''

''Right, small change.'' She tried to figure out how an interesting research project had turned into a weapon. ''Could someone have sabotaged your apparatus, so you'd get an electric shock when you exceeded certain parameters?''

''No one knows what I'm working on besides a few key government executives and a couple of people at Randolph. Everybody at my place who's in on the deal has a top-secret clearance. As for outside interference—nobody's compromised our alarm systems here at the house.''

Jo sighed. She'd wanted Cam to come up with a scientific rationale for the strange experience, because that was preferable to her other theory. ''What do *you* think is going on?'' she asked.

He tapped his thumb against his lips, and she waited tensely. ''You saw a ball of energy and a face.''

''Yes.''

''You're sure it wasn't a random pattern that reminded you of human features?''

''The features were wavering, but it looked like a man. Cam, it's the ghost who's haunting this house, isn't it? When you were talking about an anomalous matter-energy transfer, you meant something like this!''

"Not quite like *this*. When I was running the experiment, I saw an image that looked vaguely human. But I thought I was stressed out. Or that there was some logical explanation for what occurred."

Jo gnawed at her lower lip. "It only happened once? You don't think your brother or your father could have come back from—uh—the other side to give you a message? And something went wrong?"

"No. What about *your* ghost?"

"I haven't *seen* anything. But after I came home from the hospital, I started feeling his presence. Like I told you."

"It didn't start happening until after you were shot?" Cam clarified.

Jo nodded. "I used to be skeptical of people who said they'd seen a ghost—until my friend, Laura Roswell, tangled with one."

"Yeah. Wasn't she haunted by a girl who'd been murdered and wanted her to solve the case?" he recalled. "You may think I wasn't taking you seriously, but I did have Jason check out your question about someone being murdered here. He didn't find anything."

"Why didn't you tell me?"

"I only got the report when he phoned tonight."

"You must have some hypothesis about why the ghost appeared."

"The best I can come up with is that he's a spirit who existed as pure energy, and somehow he got pulled into the field I was generating. Maybe I disturbed his rest with my experiments." He sighed. "I was hoping he'd go back where he came from. I guess I was being optimistic."

"There's still my theory about Art Nugent." She gasped as an important detail came back to her. "You were the one who foiled his plan. What if he still wants me and hates you? What if he's reaching out for us from the grave?"

"Maybe you'd better stop watching the sci-fi channel."

"I don't." She glanced at the closed door. "You can make a joke about it if you want. We both know there was something out in the lab."

Cam sighed. He went to the desk and picked up the phone. After a moment, he replaced the receiver. "No dial tone. The energy surge must have shorted out the line."

"Or *he* did it. Is the rest of your communications equipment in the lab?" Jo asked.

"Yeah."

Jo took a step toward the door.

Seeing her intent, Cam grabbed her by the shoulders. "Don't you even think about going out there!"

"Do you have any better suggestion?"

He gestured toward a control box in the wall beside his desk. "You said you felt a presence but never saw anything. Okay, I'll concede we're dealing with something we can't explain. For lack of any better terminology, we'll call him a ghost. I think he's been feeding off the energy generated by my experiment, which is why he materialized in the lab. If I use the emergency shutoff, it should pull his plug again."

Jo nodded, praying it was true. As Cam threw switches, she could hear the lab equipment shutting down. She almost expected to hear some kind of shriek, as well. But there was nothing remotely ghostly.

After thirty seconds of silence, Cam turned the knob and opened the door a crack.

Jo tensed. When nothing happened, he enlarged the opening.

She watched, almost deafened by a pulse pounding in her ears. But the room beyond their refuge was as silent and empty as a church in the middle of the week. "You were right. He's gone," she breathed.

Cam took a step forward.

"Wait!" Jo grabbed his hand, and they advanced slowly across the tile floor together. She glanced nervously around. The lab remained still and silent.

Striding to the machinery, Cam checked the dials.

Jo tugged on his elbow. "Come on."

"Wait a minute. I want to run some tests. Maybe I can feed him a little energy and figure out how much power it takes to make him materialize."

A wave of cold swept over her. "No way! We don't know who he is, and we're getting out of here while we still can."

"Jo—"

"Cam, I understand the thirst for knowledge, but don't press your luck." She tugged on his hand, trying to pull him toward the door.

When he took in the anxious expression on her face, he capitulated. "Okay."

It wasn't until they'd exited into the hallway that Jo could breathe normally. "I think our next stop is the emergency room at Sinai Hospital."

He whirled toward her. "Sweetheart, what is it? Do you need to sit down?"

Jo managed a laugh. "I'm fine. *You're* the one who wasn't breathing forty minutes ago."

"But—"

"Come on, Cam. You're an intelligent man. You know you should be checked out in case you need some kind of treatment."

"What are we going to say happened—that a ghost attacked me?"

"No. That you had a severe electric shock from your lab equipment. That won't exactly be a lie."

Finally he sighed. "Okay."

Jo LAY IN BED, awake. There was no way she could sleep. Too much had happened this evening.

Cam lay breathing evenly. He'd been exhausted when they'd returned from the hospital, and went right to bed.

Jo got up and pulled on a robe. After making sure Cam hadn't awakened, she went downstairs. In the den she booted her computer, called up her Randolph investigation file and began to type in Cam's revelations about his secret government project along with questions his explanation raised.

Certainly the research put a new spin on things. What if this whole series of incidents—including the so-called ghost—were an elaborate trick to get her to unwittingly pass confidential information to the wrong people? What if someone had figured out how to project ghost-like images into their house? And the images then drew energy from Cam's equipment, confusing his results.

Jo clicked her teeth in frustration. Sheez, was she making a terrible mistake trying to handle this alone so Cam would end up without any help except from his overconfident wife? Was that what they *wanted* her to do?

But if that was the case, why arouse her suspicions in the first place? It didn't make sense.

She was deep in thought when the all-too-familiar feeling of being watched overtook her, and her whole body froze. This time she was sure it wasn't Cam standing in back of her. This was like before, when the ghost had come to her.

Only now she pictured a ball of fire glowing in the air behind her the way it had in Cam's lab. Fear made her palms grow clammy as she pictured the way the ball had turned into an arrow aimed straight for Cam's back.

It took a lot of willpower to make herself turn around. Relieved and surprised, she stared intently at the empty air.

But this wasn't like in the lab. Away from Cam's equipment, the ghost couldn't start any fireworks. Could he? And he'd never attacked *her.* Only Cam.

Still, it took several moments before she could breath somewhat normally again. Even without any visual proof, she knew their uninvited visitor was in the room with her. Watching and waiting. "Who are you? Art Nugent?" she asked in a shaky voice. "Did you come back to punish Cam for saving me?"

There was no answer.

"Go away and leave us alone."

He still didn't reply. Probably he couldn't. Ghosts couldn't talk. But he didn't leave, either. She was certain of that.

"If you aren't Art Nugent, why did you hurt Cam?" she asked.

An answer flooded back—a wave of anger so strong that she cringed. And she realized that earlier he'd been acting like a jealous lover who goes berserk and shoots his rival.

"How did you get here?"

You know. I came from the afterlife. The words stole into her mind as if he'd whispered in her ear. But she couldn't trust them. Maybe they'd bubbled up from her own subconscious because she was so anxious for explanations.

She sat unmoving, her mind swimming in deep confusion. Slowly a compulsion crept over her and became so strong that it was impossible not to act. She needed to look at the computer screen. Afraid of what she was going to see, she swiveled the chair back to its previous position.

Nothing was on the monitor except what she'd been writing, and she breathed a little sigh of relief. Then the cursor skittered to the right as if someone was holding down the space bar.

Her gaze shot to the keyboard. Nothing moved. Yet the cursor jumped again.

"Stop it! Stop playing with me," she shouted.

The invisible computer operator didn't answer, yet she felt him gliding up behind her, crowding close to her body like a man making a move on a woman.

"No! Get away from me."

Fingers seemed to brush against the back of her neck as if to gentle her. Yet the effect was just the opposite. A shiver started at her neck and went all the way down her spine. She would have jumped out of her chair if she could have made her arms and legs move.

Paralyzed, she sat staring straight ahead as if she were being held in place and commanded to attend the computer screen. It was several seconds before she realized that something was happening on the monitor. As she looked on in amazement, a white letter slowly began to form against the blue background, not as if it were being typed by a person, but as if it were being built up bit by painful bit.

Watching the phenomenon was like looking at a message that was coming into being out of smoke or mist. First a *C* took form. It was followed by an *A*. Then an *R* to spell out the word *CAR* in capital letters.

Seconds ticked by as she sat with her heart pounding.

"What does it mean?" she whispered.

Currents stirred in the room as if a window had opened, letting in a cold wind. As the air swirled around her, she felt his ghostly touch again. On her hair. On her face. On her lips. Across her breasts. She gasped. It was as if he wanted to be her lover. As if he'd made her a present of the word on the computer screen and was demanding his reward.

She didn't understand what was happening. But this time fear released her. Bolting from the chair she dashed from the room and sprinted up the stairs, her heart pounding as she waited for him to follow.

Chapter Six

He didn't follow her into the bedroom. Not this time. She was pretty sure of that. But she lay awake a good part of the night huddled next to Cam, longing to wake him and yet knowing she had to let him get his strength back.

The next morning when she opened her eyes, he was still sleeping soundly beside her in their king-size bed. She reached to stroke her hand against his cheek but drew back before she made contact with his flesh. He never slept this late, which meant he needed to rest. So she settled for watching him, admiring the twin half circles of his dark lashes, the strong line of his jaw and the innocence of his mouth when he was relaxed.

Despite her resolve, she was tempted to brush her lips against his and slide her hand down his body to wake him up in a way they'd both enjoy. Instead she dragged in a shaky little breath and rolled to her back. She and Cam were alone. A man and woman in the privacy of their own bedroom. Yet she half expected to see the apparition of a man leaning against the wall, watching them intently.

She grimaced. Last night as she'd lain awake in the darkness listening to Cam's peaceful breathing, she'd been forced into some heavy-duty speculating about the evening's events.

Although the ghost had been in the lab before, he'd only attacked Cam when he'd been about to make love to her. Maybe that was a coincidence. Maybe it wasn't. Later their uninvited houseguest had come on to her. There was no other way she could interpret his behavior. It was as if he yearned for her and was jealous of Cam.

Until she knew something more, she couldn't endanger her husband by getting intimate. She eased out of bed and stood with her hands pressed to her sides, confused and frightened, unable to cope with what she'd just been thinking. Quietly she went into her dressing room. After pulling on sweatpants and a shirt, she tiptoed into the hall.

As she descended the steps, she tensed, wondering if *he* were waiting for her. But nothing swept up the stairs to wrap her in invisible arms or cut off her breath with invisible lips. The presence that had written on the computer screen the night before was keeping its distance.

Had she been in such bad shape that she'd conjured up an illusion? She should have printed the page so she'd have some proof.

Still, as Jo made her way down the hall, her steps became slower and slower as she got closer to the site of her late-night encounter. Standing just outside the door to the office, she peered inside. The room was empty. But then she'd never seen the ghost except when Cam had turned on his lab equipment.

Teeth clenched, she stepped into the room. When nothing out of the ordinary happened, she crossed the rug. The computer was still on, and she thanked God Cam hadn't woken up first and come in here.

After a quick glance over her shoulder, she turned back to the file. The word *CAR* was right where she left it.

Letting out the breath she'd been holding, she made a hard copy of the screen. Her first thought was to show it to Cam. But as she lifted the paper from the printer and saw the rest of what was on it, she realized discussing this with her husband wasn't an option.

She was pacing back and forth between the desk and the window when the phone rang. Whirling, she snatched the receiver out of its cradle.

"Expecting someone important?" It was Mike Lancer, the P.I. she'd contacted after she'd received the roses.

"I didn't want to wake Cam."

"I thought he got up with the farmers."

"We had a late night," she said in a tone of voice designed to put an end to that line of discussion.

"I've got some information for you."

"Good."

"It's about the car."

Jo gasped, her gaze drilling in to the piece of paper clutched in her hand.

"You okay?" Mike asked.

"Yes. What about the car?"

"It's just shown up in a junkyard in Jessup."

"A junkyard? What kind of shape is it in, or do I really want to know?"

"I haven't seen it, but I'm on my way out there. Can you meet me?"

"Yes." He gave her the address, which Jo took down on the sheet of paper she was still holding. After hanging up, she stared again at the word *she* hadn't typed last night. Was it an outlandish coincidence that the ghost had tried to tell her something about the car? Or did he actually have precognition?

Quickly she scribbled a note for Cam telling him that she had urgent business that wouldn't keep. Forgetting that the doctor hadn't given her permission to drive, she closed the file, grabbed her purse and started for the garage.

But when she pulled open the connecting door and tried to step through, she met some kind of invisible resistance—like the force field that sealed off the brig on the starship *Enterprise*.

"Now what the hell are you trying to pull?" she demanded, channeling fear into anger.

Again she tried to push through the doorway. This time, the response was more personal. Unseen hands grabbed her hip and shoulder and thrust her backward several feet into the hallway. Panting, she struggled to keep him from sensing her terror. "I think you need some serious attitude adjustment!"

Silence hung heavy in the air, giving away nothing. Handicapped because she couldn't see who was restraining her, she tried to wiggle out of his clutches.

But she made no further progress into the garage. And when she slapped repeatedly at his invisible appendages, the ghostly gatekeeper turned violent. Lifting her off her feet, he pushed her backward with the force of a hundred-mile-an-hour gale. Her hair whipped around her face, and wind roared in her ears, as she sailed through the air.

"Wha—?" Jo gasped as her back hit the wall, the impact painfully jarring both her recent incision and her head. Moaning, she crumpled over and clutched her chest.

When she heard heavy footsteps racing toward her, she cringed. What was he going to do to her now?

"Jo?"

She looked and saw Cam, dressed in sweatpants and a T-shirt, sprinting down the hall. As she stared up at him in confusion, he crouched over her, his hands tender and urgent on her shoulders. "What happened? Honey, are you okay?"

She struggled to catch her breath and clear her head.

"Did you get dizzy? Did you fall? I thought you weren't supposed to go out by yourself."

"The ghos..."

"The ghost? Now what the hell is he up to?" With no other focus for his anger, Cam turned and faced the open garage door. "You son of a bitch," he growled. "Leave my wife alone!"

The door slammed firmly shut.

"He doesn't want me to leave the house," Jo whispered.

"Tell me what happened."

"I was going to get your car," she blurted before realizing she hadn't meant to be that specific.

"Was that the police who called?"

"My friend Mike Lancer," she said, feeling as if she were sinking deeper into a hole she'd just dug.

Cam looked surprised and not entirely pleased. "What's he got to do with this?"

When Jo didn't come up with an immediate answer, he focused on the computer printout in her hand.

Reflexively she tried to slip it behind her back. But he grabbed her wrist, pried her fingers open and took possession of the paper.

"Don't." She tried to snatch back the incriminating evidence, but he moved out of her grasp and scanned the text. "What the hell is this?"

"Notes," she said weakly, hoping the dim light hid the panic in her eyes.

"I can see that. Notes on Randolph Electronics—on the conversation we had last night, in fact. What did you do, come right down to the office and enter them in a secret log?"

Jo swallowed hard. "I . . . I wanted a record of what happened."

He scowled at the header. "This is page six of some existing document. Try telling me the truth for a change."

She cringed away from his fierce gaze and the pressure of his hand on her arm. "I . . . can't. Why don't we try to figure out why the ghost attacked me?"

His face turned bleak and hard. "I think we have to deal with this first."

Some part of her still tried to resist. "Cam . . . I—"

"You know," he interrupted sharply. "I've been driving myself crazy trying to figure out why you were sneaking around, doing something you didn't want me to know about the day you were almost killed."

"I wasn't intending to get shot."

"Are you in some kind of trouble? Is somebody blackmailing you into spying on me?" he persisted. "Is that it?"

Unable to speak, unable to meet his bleak gaze, she shook her head in vigorous denial.

"Jo, it's hard to believe that what you're hiding from me is worse than what I've been imagining."

"I'd never betray you," she said thickly.

His voice remained uncompromising. "I've got to know what's going on. And if I have to hack my way into your computer to find out, I will."

She knew it wasn't an idle threat. Cam had always stayed cool until he was pushed past a certain limit. Then he took whatever action he thought was necessary. In a way, it was a relief that he had lifted the decision out of her hands. Finally she didn't have to carry this terrible burden by herself.

"All right," she capitulated.

His grim expression softened as he helped her to her feet and waited to see if she was still in pain. When he was satisfied that she could walk, he led her back to her office at a fairly rapid clip.

Seating himself at the desk like a captain taking command of a vessel, he looked at her expectantly. "What's your password?"

"Your birthday."

"Great!"

He turned his total attention to the computer; she slumped onto the couch. The decision might be out of her hands, yet that didn't lessen her fear for her husband's safety—or her growing jitters as she waited for his reaction to the notes and her investigation.

He said nothing, and when she couldn't cope with the rigid set of his shoulders or the silence in the room, she closed her eyes and leaned her head back.

Finally she heard Cam's chair swivel around, and her eyes snapped open. His gaze pinned her to the couch. "Why didn't you come to me as soon as you got the first anonymous note? Didn't you trust me?"

The tears she'd been struggling to hold back leaked down her cheeks, and she looked at him pleadingly. "I decided to tell you after I got home from the hospital, then the card came with the roses, and I thought they were watching me—even in the house," she said, chokingly.

"What roses?"

She realized she'd been too upset to enter *that* crucial piece of information into the computer file where it belonged. "They're out here." Taking Cam by the hand, she led him to the laundry room and over to the cabinet where she'd hidden the evidence.

The silver bowl with the flowers was still inside, only now they were dry and limp as month-old funeral offerings. Jo stared at them in distaste.

"Where did these come from?"

"The same place as the other notes," she whispered. She felt around in the box and found the crumpled card, which she silently handed to Cam.

He cursed when he read it. She thought he was going to pick up the arrangement and toss it against the wall. Instead he put it back in the cabinet and slammed the door shut. "When did it arrive?"

"The day my friends came over. In the morning. I called the florist, but they didn't have a record of the order. And Mike checked with the deliveryman. When he found the flowers in the truck, he thought someone had forgotten to put them on the delivery list."

He looked at her with new understanding and a softening in his eyes. "No wonder you were in such bad shape that day."

She gulped and took a small step toward him. For weeks she'd felt so alone and helpless as she grappled with forces she didn't understand. Now she could finally turn to Cam the way she should have in the first place. It felt good. Right.

"I needed you. I didn't know what to do," she whispered.

Her name broke from his lips as he closed the remaining distance between them in a couple of giant strides. He folded her in his arms and cradled her against his chest. Tears in her eyes, she clung to him with all her strength. He stroked her hair, comforting and reassuring her that everything was going to be all right.

"Cam, I love you," she murmured. "I know I made a mistake, but I was trying to protect you."

"I know that, honey. I should have trusted you. I'm sorry you had to cope with something like this on your own," he muttered, holding her so tightly that she could hardly draw in a full breath.

The words were a balm, wiping away the deep, throbbing pain of the past few months. "It's not your fault," she soothed.

"Of course it is. Someone's screwing around with my company, and you've gotten sucked into the mess. In fact, it looks like they set a trap for you." He led her back into the den.

"We don't know that for sure. Maybe I was just in the wrong place at the wrong time. Those car jackers could have been scouting around for a victim. When they saw me, they may have figured I was an easy target."

He sighed. "Perhaps, but I think it's more complicated than that."

"I keep wishing I could remember exactly what happened, that if I could bring the attack into focus, it would make a big difference."

"Maybe you never will."

She hated to admit that possibility, but he might be right.

"Let's get back to what happened a little while ago. The ghost didn't let you leave the house. That's very interesting."

Jo nodded. They had finally come full circle—back to the spook who was escalating his campaign against them.

"I'd like to know whose side he's on."

"Last night, he, uh, touched me."

"What?"

She was instantly sorry she'd mentioned it.

"Where?"

"On the back of the neck, and, uh, my face."

Cam's eyes narrowed. "That's a new development."

"It was no big deal," she lied, and hurried to change the subject. "He wrote me something on the computer."

"When were you going to get around to telling me?"

"I couldn't because it's the last word at the end of the file you just read."

"Right."

Cam marched over to the computer screen and jabbed his finger against the word *CAR*. "I thought you might have typed it after you talked to Lancer—to remind yourself to add some notes later."

Jo described how the letters had appeared on the monitor.

He swung his gaze around the room as if inviting direct contact with their unseen correspondent. "I guess he's better than a Ouija board. But I'd like to know what he really wants from us."

Jo nodded tightly, unsure how to respond to the sarcasm in his voice.

"I'm sorry. I'm not handling this very well." He sighed. "See what happens if you ask him nicely."

Jo straightened but kept hold of Cam's hand. "We want to communicate with you. Would you please send us another message?"

Nothing happened, except that she felt a flush creep into her cheeks.

"Maybe we should call the psychic hotline," Cam muttered under his breath.

Jo gave Cam a pleading look.

He scowled but said nothing more.

She cleared her throat. "If you're really here, then the three of us have to come to some kind of understanding."

She thought she'd failed, until she felt Cam stiffen beside her. Following the direction of his gaze, she saw that the cursor on the computer screen was blinking oddly again.

Jo grabbed Cam's hand. He nodded, but neither of them broke the silence in the room.

Like the night before, a letter began to form. As Jo watched, the hair on the back of her neck prickled, and she felt Cam's tension. The letter resolved into an *N*, and Jo's excitement mounted. She'd asked for a message, and the ghost was complying. The *N* was followed by an *R*, then a *G* and something that looked like the start of a *Y* with the second arm missing. They waited for half a minute, but that was all they got.

"*N-R-G-Y?*" Jo spelled the letters. "What's that supposed to mean?"

"It could mean anything," Cam snapped. "He's a regular Delphic oracle."

"A what?"

"In ancient Greece, people would travel hundreds of miles to consult the priests at the temple of Delphi to learn of important future events, like whether they were going to win a war or inherit a kingdom. The priests were masters of serving up prophecies so ambiguous that whatever happened they could claim they'd been right."

She tapped the letters on the screen. "When you say this out loud, it sounds like 'energy' without the *E*s."

"I suppose. Or he's having fun with us." Cam growled as he confronted the monitor. "How about it, Mr. Magic? Are you going to play it straight?"

The cursor flared for an instant as if the ghost had answered with an angry rejoinder.

"Cam, he's going to think you're not serious."

"Oh, I'm serious all right." Getting up, he hauled Jo to her feet and toward the door.

"Where are we going?"

"The lab—where we have a better chance of communicating."

She dug in her heels. "No."

"Oh, yes. I'm tired of tiptoeing around my own house, trying to guess how this turkey wants me to behave."

"But last night he could have killed you."

"I think he's telling us he needs power to do anything substantial, so I'll only give him a little."

She couldn't stop Cam from dragging her downstairs, so she went along without resisting, determined to stay close to him. But as she watched him start up the equipment, a terrible feeling of tension built in her chest. Something important was going to happen. She sensed it. She prayed that it was going to be good, not bad.

"You won't hurt him again," she whispered, unsure of exactly where to direct the plea. Or whether it would have any effect.

"What?" Cam snapped, turning momentarily from one of the machines.

"I—nothing."

He walked toward another piece of equipment, and Jo felt the air in the room stir as if it were alive. She sensed unseen forces seething with impatience. Quietly she moved closer to Cam. When she put her hand on his shoulder, she felt his muscles jump. Yet his face looked cool as he worked.

Jo felt her own pulse rate speed up, as if there were a direct connection between the equipment and her physiology. She wanted to shout at Cam to stop. She knew he wouldn't listen.

He turned the dial he'd been twisting the night before. Jo held her breath. For several seconds, nothing strange happened. Then, in the center of the room, the air began to shimmer like waves of intense heat rising from a desert plain. Yet the temperature in the lab hadn't changed by so much as a degree. Jo gasped and took an involuntary step back, but she was unable to look away from the place where the molecules wavered and rippled.

Beside her, Cam made a muffled exclamation.

She didn't realize she'd forgotten to breathe until her burning lungs forced her to exhale and draw in more oxygen. Where the air in the lab flickered, a gossamer image began to form. At first it was blurry and indistinct, but she could make out a man wearing casual slacks and a rumpled button-down shirt. He was standing in a very self-contained pose with his arms folded across his chest. The clothes and the posture made her heart begin to thump. As she watched, his form became sharper, more real. Half eager, half afraid, she slowly raised her gaze up the length of his body to his face. His hair was light colored and close cropped. His eyes were deep set under straight brows. His lips were thin and pressed into a set line as he regarded her steadily.

"Oh, my God," she wheezed. "It's Skip!"

Skip O'Malley, the man she'd been married to for eight years. The man who'd been shot and killed before she'd ever met Cameron Randolph.

Her knees buckled, and she grabbed for the wall.

Chapter Seven

The ghost's face contorted, and he shouted something urgent, but the words didn't reach Jo. Nothing could have reached her through the roaring sound in her ears that threatened to sweep away her sanity.

She stared at him, through him, overwhelmed by a sense of regret, of loss, of sadness so strong that it was more than any human being should have to bear.

Memory slammed into her hard and fast like a freight train, knocking the breath from her body in a tortured rush, leaving her raw and unprotected and unprepared to cope with what she was feeling.

She moaned wordlessly as the room around her faded to gray. Alone and frightened, she was catapulted back to the day her husband had been killed. Struggling to grapple with the unthinkable.

"Oh, Skip."

He didn't answer. He'd never had a chance to answer.

That morning they'd had a fight because she was convinced the case he was working on was dangerous and that he needed to call in the police. But he'd been too macho to take her advice.

She'd been right. He'd been wrong. The decision to shadow a pair of hired killers had cost him his life. And he'd died with her angry words echoing in her ears along with the hollow sound of gunfire.

"Forgive me. It wasn't like that. I loved you," she whispered. Then with a ragged little sob, she raised her hand to her lips and pressed hard.

Unable to support herself, she sagged against the wall. Strong arms were there to reach for her. But she was barely aware of them, barely aware of being eased into a chair. A long time later, she heard someone calling her name.

"Jo? Jo?"

Gradually she realized Cam was speaking to her, had been speaking in a low voice that sounded barely under control. It took a tremendous effort to focus on his face. As she stared into his troubled gray eyes, she remembered where she was. And what they had come down here to do. Communicate with the ghost who was turning their lives upside down.

But the ghost was Skip.

Her head swung toward the otherworldly image. He was still standing in the corner of the room, watching her with an intensity that made her heart threaten to pound its way through her chest. He didn't come any closer. But last night he had touched her, kissed her. And she hadn't known who he was.

How had that made him feel?

Unable to deal with the look of regret etched on his face, she wrenched her gaze away and sat huddled in the chair, stunned, disoriented.

"Jo?" Cam said again, his fingers digging into her shoulders. The naked pain in his voice reached her as nothing else had. She had to pull herself together. For him. For them. She had to go on.

No. She *had* pulled herself together. She *had* gone on. Skip had been dead for ten years. And she'd forged a bond with a man she loved more than life itself.

She looked around the room. Cam's lab. In the house they'd built together. With a terrible effort, she brought her mind back to reality, to herself—to the person she'd grown into since Skip had died. To the woman she'd become since she'd met Cam and merged her heart and soul with his.

The feeling of sadness, of loss, of missed opportunities, faded into the background where it had to stay. Only she knew she was never going to be quite the same as she had been before they'd come down here and Cam had turned that knob.

"The ghost is Skip? You mean your dead husband? The guy whose name is still on the door of your detective agency?" Cam asked as if he were praying that it wasn't true. "He's the one who's been dogging us?"

She nodded.

"Where did he come from? Did you bring him?"

"Yes. In a way," she whispered, still dazed by the incomprehensible.

His face turned dark, and he looked away from her.

She grabbed his arm, as if physical contact could help him understand how she felt, what she was going through. "I didn't ask him. He followed me back from the tunnel." Even as she said the words, she realized they were true. A missing piece of her recent memory had come back.

"You talked about a tunnel in the hospital."

"Did I?" Her emotions roiled again as Skip moved into her line of vision as if determined to be an active participant in this scene. She looked from one man to the other—her flesh-and-blood husband and the one whose image was like a faded color transparency projected into the middle of the room.

She gulped. "I—I left my body and went up to that bright light and the tunnel you've heard people talk about."

Cam nodded tightly.

"Skip was there, waiting for me."

She wondered how Cam would react. He looked as if he accepted her explanation.

Moving in closer, he held on to her more tightly, as if he was afraid she'd leave him again. "When I found you, your heart wasn't beating, and I was sure I'd gotten there too late. Then suddenly I felt your pulse, and at first I couldn't believe my senses. It was literally as if you'd left your body and then returned."

"Skip sent me back—because it wasn't my time yet."

"That was very gracious of him."

The sharp edge of Cam's voice tore at her.

"Help me," she whispered, praying that he'd understand how hard this was for her.

"I won't let him hurt you again," he growled.

That wasn't what she'd meant at all. "He doesn't want to hurt me."

"How do you know?"

She shook her head. "I just know."

"Then why did he slam you into the wall when you tried to leave the house a while ago?"

Skip gestured wildly and said something she couldn't hear.

Jo looked beseechingly at Cam. "I can't explain what happened in the hall."

"Did he tell you he was coming back to disrupt our lives?" Cam asked.

Jo shook her head, her eyes pleading with Cam to ease up on her.

A low, rumbling vibration started in the air around the ghost. His image shimmered violently, and his face contorted again. Although he looked as if he was shouting at the top of his lungs, no sound reached them.

"You want to say something in your own defense?" Cam growled.

For several seconds, the ghostly image became more solid, but it was obvious that he couldn't sustain the effect. He nodded and glared at Cam.

Cam glared back.

"If we adjust the output of the machine, would Skip be able to talk?" Jo asked.

"I don't know. There's no spec sheet on powering up the undead."

Skip bared his teeth in a silent snarl at the choice of words.

Cam got to his feet and surveyed the lab equipment. Then with a resigned look on his face he crossed the room and began to adjust some of the dials, glancing from the machinery to the specter as he made various corrections. Slowly he boosted the output, and the outlines of Skip's body became sharper and a bit more opaque. The apparition held out his hand and looked at it, flexing the fingers. Then his lips began to move again.

This time Jo heard his voice and shivered. It was thin and tinny—like an old phonograph record. But the words were distinct. "You bastard." He flung the words at Cam.

"Wait a damn minute!" Cam shot back as he lunged forward.

Acting on instinct, Jo jumped in front of him and blocked his path. "He hurt you yesterday. He can do it again. And you can't do anything to him."

Cam stopped, his hands clenched into fists. "I can shut off his power."

"And we won't find out why he's here and what he wants."

"I know what he wants!"

"Do you?"

He didn't answer, but she could see he was making an effort to get control of himself. She turned toward the ghost. "Promise me you won't do anything to Cam."

"I can take care of myself," Cam growled.

"Promise," Jo repeated.

"Okay, Red, for you," Skip rumbled.

Jo's heart contracted at the familiar endearment. No one had called her that since...Skip had died. She sent him a silent plea for understanding, and his expression softened.

Still she felt like a referee in a wrestling match as she steered Cam toward a neutral corner. She knew things had gone badly when the two men had worked together on a case years before she and Cam had met, and death hadn't improved the relationship. God, she wasn't up to acting as a buffer between them. But she was the only one who could do it. Somehow she willed her voice to sound calm and steady.

"I think we need to change the direction of the discussion."

Nobody raised an objection.

"Why did you stop me from leaving the house this morning?" she asked Skip.

"You were going to his car, and he told his buddy Jason on the phone that anyone who fools with the equipment in it will get blown up!"

"You were listening to my conversation?" Cam accused.

"Right. Because I'll use every tool at my disposal to protect Jo. *That's* why I came back with her, since you asked."

Cam jumped on the previous point of contention. "Well, Mr. Private Detective, you didn't understand what you were hearing about the car. The vehicle's not going to blow up. If someone tries to operate the equipment without the correct computer authorization, the hardware will fuse," Cam enunciated carefully. "Why don't you just butt out of our lives, and go back where you came from."

"I may not have pegged all the jargon in your conversation, but I understand the big picture. Your stupid scientific experiments have put Jo in mortal danger. And I'm not leaving until I can figure out how to save her."

"Now wait a damn minute. She's my wife, and *I* can take care of her."

"Oh, yeah. Well, she got popped in the chest because someone's trying to steal your whiz-bang wave compressor." Skip gestured toward the bank of equipment on the far wall.

"How do *you* know that?"

"Deductive reasoning. You're about to make a breakthrough on the cutting edge of technology, and someone else wants to reap the rewards."

"Nobody knows I'm working on an energy compressor besides the Defense Department. Jim Crowley's the project manager, and he's classified it top secret.''

"But you've conferred with half a dozen people in your company.''

"Who all have top-secret clearances. I trust them implicitly.''

"Well, someone's been running off at the mouth.''

"Who?'' Cam demanded.

"I don't have enough information to figure that out yet. But I do know Jo is still in danger.''

"You have some facts to back that up?''

"She just told you about the flowers some bozo sent. And while you were sleeping, she was going to make herself a target again. For all I know, the bad guys arranged for Mike Lancer to locate your fancy wheels so he could call up Jo, and she could go charging off half-cocked.''

"I don't go charging off half-cocked,'' Jo interjected.

"That was always one of your big weaknesses.''

"You're the one who trained her,'' Cam said, jumping in. "And you're the one who got himself killed investigating a case you should have left to the police.''

Jo sucked in a strangled breath as the terrible memory slammed her again.

Neither of the men noticed. They were regarding each other with barely controlled hostility.

Feeling as if she were being torn in two, Jo stared from one to the other. She was so badly shaken that she could hardly think. "Please, this isn't getting us anywhere,'' she pleaded.

Both husbands turned toward her. Both of them looked troubled and uncertain.

She focused on Cam, silently begging him not to fly off the handle again. When he nodded almost imperceptibly, she took several steps toward Skip, stopping when she was a few feet from his image.

His total concentration was on her, and she felt both relieved and guilty. She was committed to her marriage with Cam. Yet some part of her would always love Skip O'Malley—would always remember the pain of losing him and regret the angry words she'd flung at him that morning.

Their eyes met. Hers were watery. His were full of pain and confusion. He started to reach for her. When he remembered he couldn't touch her, he grimaced and folded his arms across his chest again. She felt her stomach knot painfully. Lord, this was so hard!

Somehow she kept herself from glancing back at Cam to see how he was reacting. She didn't have to see his face. She knew he couldn't stand seeing her with the man she'd once loved. Especially when he'd been so unsure of her motives—and her loyalty.

She stood there, feeling as if she were being stretched on a medieval torture rack. She wanted to turn and throw herself into Cam's arms. Yet she couldn't do that, either—not with Skip watching and looking so sad.

"You've changed," the ghost said, making it as much an accusation as an observation.

"Of course. I've...it's been ten years."

"Your life is pretty different."

"Yes."

"You—"

She didn't allow him to keep the focus on her. "You've changed, too."

"Oh, yeah?"

She tried to project an aura of calm, to make it clear that she wasn't being judgmental. "In the tunnel, after I was shot, you seemed so selfless, so concerned about my welfare," she said very quietly, as if they were having a totally private conversation. "But back here you're doing things that are making me upset, things that come across as destructive."

He looked uncomfortable. "Up there it's different."

"How?" she prompted, hoping Cam had enough self-control not to interfere.

"Your perspective changes. You're not all wound up in your own needs. But when I followed you back to earth, I guess I started buying back into all the things people want for themselves."

She swallowed painfully. The look in his eyes proclaimed how much he longed to be with her, to please her, and she wasn't prepared to deal with the implications.

"I shouldn't have attacked your husband," he muttered.

"I was so frightened."

"I know. I saw you," he admitted in a raw voice. "When you're not used to having badass thoughts, they can flare up like...like an erupting volcano. I'm sorry."

Jo was silent for several seconds, vividly aware that Cam was waiting for her response, too.

"I accept the apology," she finally whispered. The words hung in the air, filling the room. Desperate for some less-personal focus to the discussion, she asked the first question that came into her head. "How are you getting your information about the wave compressor and everything else?"

"Mostly I'm the proverbial fly on the wall. One thing about being a ghost, it makes surveillance a heck of a lot easier. I was reading your computer file over your shoulder last night.''

''I know.''

Cam jumped back into the conversation with both feet. ''So you've been eavesdropping on both of us.''

''If that's what you want to call it.''

''What would *you* call it?''

Skip ignored the question. ''It's a damn good thing I'm here, since neither one of you has the whole picture.''

''Oh?' Cam challenged.

Skip turned to Jo. ''He may be stringing you the line that he trusts his employees, but he's having Zacharias do a security check on everyone at Randolph Electronics who might have knowledge of the Pulsar project.''

''That's proprietary information!'' Cam growled.

''Not when it affects my wife's safety.''

''*My* wife,'' Cam reminded him. ''And I can damn well protect her.''

Jo swung toward Cam. ''What else are you keeping from me?''

Instead of responding, he snapped, ''It looks like Skip's accomplished his mission—driving a wedge between the two of us.''

''That's not my mission, Mr. Hotshot Inventor. I'm here to guard Jo.''

To Jo's everlasting relief, the phone chose that moment to ring. Bolting to the desk, she snatched up the receiver. ''Hello?''

It was Mike Lancer. ''Jo. I thought you were on your way out the door.''

''I've gotten stuck in the middle of an, uh, domestic crisis. What's wrong?''

"The salvage company won't let me claim your car because I don't have any proof of ownership, and it's scheduled for the wrecking compactor within the hour."

"I'll be right there."

Hanging up, she turned back to man and ghost. "That was Mike Lancer. If there's any evidence in the car, it's going to be obliterated—unless we can stop the junkyard from compacting it."

Cam blinked. "Destroying a nine-month-old Lexus? They must be out of their freaking minds."

"You got an emotional attachment to your wheels?" Skip asked.

"Hell, I can get another car. But I won't know why they wanted it unless I can examine it."

"Then let's stop them." Jo was halfway to the door before Cam called her back.

"Maybe Skip is right. Maybe it is an ambush," he said in a gritty voice. "There's no use our both walking into danger."

"I'm going with you!" she shot back.

He glanced at Skip. "I doubt your guardian angel will let you leave the house. I don't even know if he'll let *me* leave."

"*You* can do what you want," Skip said between clenched teeth.

"I'm going, too," Jo told him. "If you think you've got to protect me, you can come along."

"Don't I wish," Skip answered. "I've tried to leave this mansion of yours, but I can't get past the front door. I must be tied to the wave compressor in some way."

"Well, that's useful information," Cam muttered.

"Your husband's right about one thing. *You're* not leaving, either," Skip informed Jo.

"Mike's been at the junkyard all morning. He'd know if it's being watched."

"I don't know anything about his capabilities."

"I handpicked him for this job."

"I wish I could size him up."

Jo's chin jutted toward the ghostly image. "Well, you can't. And we're wasting time. If we want to get to the car before it's too late, we have to leave." She dragged in a deep breath. "Cam will be with me, and I'll be perfectly safe. If you interfere with us, I'll consider that a hostile act."

Skip stood planted in the center of the room, looking at her defiantly.

"I'm through arguing. You'll have to trust my judgment on this." After several seconds, Jo walked over to the wave compressor. With a trembling hand, she twisted the power switch. Skip's likeness flickered out of existence.

"He's still here. All you did was shut off the sound and fury," Cam reminded her.

"I'm hoping he realizes he can't make decisions for me," Jo countered.

Half expecting some kind of force field to block her path, she marched toward the door.

"WHICH JUNKYARD are we headed for?" Cam asked as he pulled open the door of Jo's classic Mustang.

"It's in Jessup—near the women's penitentiary."

"A choice location." With unaccustomed jerky motions, he backed out of the garage and nosed down the driveway. He didn't breathe easily until the car had pulled through the Plantation's entrance gate.

"The son of a bitch let us go," he muttered.

"He's worried about me."

"I don't need him to help me take care of you!" He hated the raw note in his voice, so he pressed his lips together.

"I know."

He tried to discount the hint of doubt he detected in her quick answer. He wanted to pull over to the side, turn her toward him and look into her eyes. Then he'd know what she was really feeling. About him. About Skip. Maybe. She'd hidden so much from him lately. Every conversation with her had made him feel as if he were standing on shifting sand, unable to get his balance.

But they had to get to Jessup as quickly as possible, so he kept his gaze glued to the windshield and his foot on the accelerator.

The car shot forward, and Jo's knuckles whitened as they gripped the edge of her seat.

He sped south, his outward attention focused intently on the road and the other vehicles. But his mind was still reeling from the scene in the lab.

Last night an apparition had attacked him. He'd been shaken to the core to find out it was Skip O'Malley—to see him standing there big as life, mocking him. He'd wanted to march across the room and cut off the ghost's power—to send him back to oblivion. But he'd known with a sick felling in his gut that merely shutting off the power wasn't going to do the trick. He had the ability to make Skip O'Malley invisible. But now that Jo's former husband was here, he couldn't make him vanish from their lives. The bastard had been lurking around the house for weeks. And he wasn't going to leave until—

Until what?

He'd said he'd returned to watch over Jo. Cam's teeth clenched. That was *his* job. To protect his wife. But what if Skip were right? What if he wasn't up to the task? Before he could get a grip on himself, the secret fear that had leapt out at him in the lab came bubbling back to the surface. What if the ghost really were the better man? O'Malley was a seasoned private detective. He knew all the angles in a case like this. And as a ghost he had access to privileged information.

What if O'Malley was the only one who really could make a difference for Jo? What if he accomplished his mission, and then did what he'd really come for?

He'd seen the way O'Malley looked at Jo. Like a lovesick bull. He wanted her back. And he was angling himself into a good position to take her.

But worse than that, he'd seen the look of anguish on Jo's face. Seen the way she was remembering her life with O'Malley.

Some kind of raw sound must have escaped from his lips, because Jo's head jerked toward him.

"Cam?"

He cleared his throat. "Which exit did you say?"

"Route 175." Her hands fluttered uncertainly. She turned to him, an imploring look on her face. "I'm sorry all this is happening."

He caught the soft edge of tears in her voice and swallowed hard. "Yeah."

She was silent for several moments. "Skip wants to help us."

"He wants to help *you*," he said much too loudly. "That's not exactly the same thing." A flood of questions and pleas threatened to burst from behind his lips. But he couldn't trust himself to say anything else or do more than keep his hands glued to the wheel.

They tightened painfully, symbolically. He was going to hang on to Jo any way he could—fighting fair or fighting dirty if he had to. Maybe when they got home he'd find some way to give the damn ghost a jolt of juice so powerful that it would send him to join the Mars probe that was lost in space.

They rode in silence for several more miles, and he found he couldn't cope with that, either. Not with Jo sitting beside him in the confined space of the Mustang. So he cast around for a safe topic. "Let's talk about the car. Whoever stole it couldn't remove my computer equipment. But they could have dumped the whole thing in the river. So why did they take it to a junkyard?"

She seemed relieved to be focusing on the case. "If they'd dumped it in a river, there's some chance it might have been found. Once it's compressed into a metal cube, there's no way anybody's going to find it."

"Yeah." Cam pressed down harder on the accelerator as he wove through the midmorning traffic. They made it to Route 175 in record time. Then, near the Baltimore-Washington Parkway, the radar detector started to beep and he had to slow down.

JO EXHALED SHARPLY as they crawled up the highway at fifty-five miles per hour. She'd been all fired up to rush off to the junkyard, and not just as an excuse to separate Cam and Skip. Really, she should be champing at the bit to get there. Yet part of her was relieved at the delay.

Because the closer they got to their goal, the more difficult it was to sit calmly in her seat and pretend she was on a normal mission to collect some evidence. She'd been shot in that car. Her blood stained the front seat.

And the thought of getting anywhere near the vehicle again was tying her stomach in knots.

Maybe they would be too late. She couldn't stop herself from feeling relieved as she pictured the Lexus crushed beyond recognition. Then guilt made her thrust the image from her mind. Cam was right. They had to examine the car. They had to find out if the computer equipment was intact. And maybe, if they got lucky, they'd find out who tried to kill her.

Finally they reached the side road where the junkyard was located.

"Turn here," she directed.

Mike was parked outside the gate, pacing back and forth on the shoulder. "Thank God," he shouted. When he trotted over and saw who was driving, his expression changed to one of surprise. "I thought your husband wasn't in on this."

"It's a long story."

From the interior of the junkyard, a grating sound stopped the conversation cold. Jo gasped as she saw a set of metal jaws hoisting the Lexus into the air.

Cam swore and pulled open the car door. "Stay with her," he called to Mike as he ran full tilt through the gate.

Chapter Eight

At the bottom of the hill, Cam veered off the gravel road that led to the office. Adrenaline pumped through his veins as he sprinted through a maze of used tires and discarded metal parts toward the spot where his sixty-thousand-dollar sports car dangled in the air like a dead mouse hanging by its tail.

It felt good to be running. Good to have a goal he might attain.

"Hey, you can't go over there," a workman yelled as Cam crashed through a chain link gate, ignoring the Danger—Do Not Enter sign.

"State inspector. Official business," he said over his shoulder as he headed for what looked like the operator's booth a hundred feet farther on. Inside he could see a guy with long hair and a Hulk Hogan physique at the controls.

"Stop! That's my car!" he shouted. The man went on pressing buttons as if he was deaf. Behind Cam, a terrible crash rent the air. His head whipped around, and he saw the Lexus falling into a rectangular metal pit. Cursing under his breath, he sprinted the last few yards to the booth.

"What the hell are you doing in here!" the hulk demanded.

"Saving my property."

"You're crazy, man." He pressed a button, and metal walls began to grind in on the doomed vehicle.

Unwilling to give up, Cam scanned the control panel and located the emergency shutoff switch. He was reaching for it when the operator jumped him from behind.

Cam had thought he was in reasonably good shape, but the hulk spun him around and away from the control panel as if he were a child's top. There was no chance of shaking off the two-hundred-pound attacker. Bearing the extra weight, Cam lunged again for the switch and somehow managed to flip it off. Immediately the machinery ground to a halt.

The hulk cursed. In the next second, Cam felt a sharp chop to the back of his head. He was still staggering under the blow when large hands reached around to choke him. With all his strength, he reared back, knocking the man against the wall once, twice. He might as well have tried to batter a rhinoceros into submission. The stranglehold only tightened. His lungs felt like a damaged nuclear reactor ready to blow. The veins on his head and neck throbbed, and his vision swam in and out of focus. He struggled to hang on to consciousness, but he knew it was going to be all over in a matter of moments. Behind him, the door slammed open.

"Cam!" Jo screamed. Then he heard metal hitting bone. Mercifully the weight slipped off his back, and a heavy body crashed to the floor.

Cam leaned against the wall, unable to do more than suck in huge drafts of air. When his vision cleared, his eyes flicked to Jo.

Her face was white, and she was clutching a crowbar like a battle-ax.

"I thought I told you to stay with Mike."

"Lucky I'm not great at taking orders." She dropped her weapon and came into his arms. "Are you all right?"

"I think so."

The control booth was deathly quiet. He could feel tremors of reaction making her shiver as they clung to each other. He hung on to her tightly—needing the contact, needing the feel of her body pressed close to his.

"Thanks." There was so much more he needed to say. But he was afraid to let it pour out, afraid that if he started he might never stop. Or worse—that she didn't want to hear it.

But in that moment of shared silent communion, she strengthened her grip.

He would have kept on holding her like that forever. But his gaze was drawn to the man who lay facedown on the floor. Probably he wouldn't be getting up anytime soon. But he wasn't going to take chances with Jo in the room.

"Come on."

He steered Jo outside. When she gave him a critical inspection, he straightened and pretended his neck and back didn't feel as if they'd been caught in a giant nut-cracker.

Back on the gravel road, they encountered Mike Lancer and a burly freckle-faced man, who introduced himself as Dwayne Ralston, the owner of the yard.

"Lancer tells me Harry was gonna crunch your vehicle," Ralston said apologetically. "Don't know how a screwup like that coulda happened. He's one of my best men, and he ain't supposed to take no jobs without the title or a release from the police."

"I told him it would be plain stupid to smash an expensive car unless it was totaled," Mike added. "But he didn't seem to care."

"Let's wake him up," Jo suggested. "And ask him what he knows."

Ralston was still muttering to himself as they reentered the control booth. Jo, who was in the lead, stopped short and gasped. "He's gone."

Cam made a quick inspection of the booth.

The man who'd been out cold only minutes before had vanished.

"How'd he get up so fast?" she asked.

"Maybe he didn't get very far," Cam suggested.

They all went back outside to search the grounds. Ralston and Lancer moved off in one direction, Cam and Jo in the other.

"WHAT IF SOMEONE ELSE hauled him out of here while we were talking to Ralston?" Jo asked as they rounded the remains of a sixties El Dorado.

"Who?"

She shrugged, and they kept on searching.

A few minutes later, she stopped in her tracks and cocked her head to the side. "Listen. Do you hear that?"

"What?"

"Someone moaned."

They both stood very still amid the rusting cars and metal debris. When the noise came again, it seemed to be emanating from the trunk of a beat-up Ford several feet away.

Jo started forward, but Cam held her back and peeked through the window. No one was inside. However, there were recent streaks in the greasy dirt around the trunk.

"Over here," he shouted.

When the other two arrived, Mike and Cam cautiously tackled the trunk. It sprang open as they pulled upward.

Jo stared at the short, dark-haired man inside, wondering if her eyes were playing tricks.

"It's not the guy who attacked me," Cam confirmed. He and Mike eased the assault victim out of the vehicle and loosened the ropes that bound his legs and wrists. Cam pulled the tape from his mouth.

"Harry," Ralston boomed. "What happened, boy?"

The young operator moaned, gingerly touching a knot on his head the size of a golf ball. "I was, uh, working the machine and something hit me right up side the head."

After a brief conversation with the youth, Ralston turned back to Cam. "I'm real sorry this happened to you folks. We'll take care of towing your car wherever you say. And I'll give you a real sweet deal on used parts."

"Just have the car delivered to Randolph Security. The address is on the card. But I'd like to look it over before we leave," Cam told him.

"You got it."

"I'll ride with them to make sure it gets there," Mike offered.

Jo gave him a grateful look. "Thanks."

When she turned around, Ralston was directing the removal of the Lexus from the wrecking chamber.

While they'd been busy, she'd been able to put aside her fears. Now she was suddenly face-to-face with the reality of the car where she'd almost died. She wanted to back away, but Cam was right beside her. More than that, she wouldn't allow herself to run just because her palms were sweating and her knees were weak. So she stood there quietly watching the car being towed forward, feeling as if she were awaiting her execution.

As soon as the car was in the open, Cam trotted forward and began to make an inspection. The sides were caved in, the bumpers were twisted and the back window had shattered, filling the rear seat with glass.

She winced as he gave a mighty yank to open the door. It screamed in protest. Cam slipped into the passenger seat and studied the dashboard.

When she heard him swear, she forced herself to come closer. "Did they get your equipment?" she asked in a strained voice.

"Someone tried to take it out. But it self-destructed as programmed." He gestured toward a blob of fused plastic.

She nodded tightly. *Get it over with. Face it.* She commanded her legs to carry her to the other side of the car.

The bullet holes in the gray metal drew her gaze like malicious eyes set in an off-balance face.

She stopped breathing as she ran her fingers over the indentations. When she felt as if her legs would no longer hold her weight, she sank onto the seat next to Cam and turned her head slightly away so he wouldn't see the panic in her eyes.

"I wasn't sure you were going to get in," he said tightly.

"Neither was I," she admitted in a low voice.

He covered her hand with his, massaging her stiff fingers. "This must be awful for you."

She nodded. "I didn't think it was going to be this bad returning to the scene of the crime."

"Are you remembering what happened?"

She gulped. "Mostly I'm just getting impressions—disjointed flashes. Except for the gun. I remember the gun pointed at me. And the terror."

"Let's get out of here."

She longed to take him up on the offer. "Let's sit still for a while. I'm feeling like I'm just on the edge of remembering something important. And if I get out of the car, it may go away." Squeezing Cam's fingers in a death grip, she leaned back and tried to empty her mind.

Just before it happened, she'd... What? Her hand linked to Cam's became the focus of her concentration. Her hand. She'd been holding something in her hand. And she'd put it down. On the seat where she was sitting now.

"It was... a roll of film," she said triumphantly.

"What?"

"I was shooting pictures of a guy sneaking around the warehouse. I used up one roll of film and loaded another. Just before the shooting started, I put the first one on the seat beside me."

Scrambling out of the car, she began to feel around the floor mat.

Cam followed suit. But they found nothing.

"They could have found it," he muttered. "Or maybe it rolled out in the scuffle."

"Maybe not." She slipped her fingers into the space where the front seat met the back rest. Wedged far down into the leather was a small cylinder. She drew it out and held it up triumphantly.

Cam smiled. "I'd like to see who you have on film."

"So would I."

EMOTIONALLY AND physically drained, Jo leaned back in the Mustang's comfortable bucket seat and closed her eyes.

"You okay?" Cam asked.

"Worn-out."

He touched her damp brow. "Too bad this had to be your first trip out since the hospital. You could have done with a little less excitement."

"Umm."

She might have kept the conversation going; instead she closed her eyes again as Cam drove toward Owings Mills. She wished her brain would shut down. But she couldn't stop her thoughts from churning. Now that they were heading home, she began to think about Skip.

Once more she relieved the shock of seeing him standing in the lab. Her former husband. A man she'd loved. A man who had died with unfinished business. As it had before, a wave of sorrow and regret swept over her. This time she was a little better prepared. This time the old grief didn't knock her off her feet. She'd lost Skip a long time ago. It was almost as if she'd been a different person back then.

It was odd to be able to see that former self with mature objectivity. It made her realize how much she'd grown and changed. She'd been so green when she'd first come to Baltimore from western Maryland. But she'd been determined to make something of herself, and she'd also been looking for adventure.

The O'Malley Detective Agency's ad for a secretary had been the first one she'd answered. She'd impressed Skip O'Malley with her business-course typing skills. It wasn't until she'd been working in his office for several months that he found out what a mess she'd made of his files. But by that time he'd gotten into the habit of discussing his cases with her. And he'd found out that she had a natural aptitude for deductive reasoning.

Jo had realized pretty quickly that her boss was attracted to her yet reluctant to make a move. However, she'd used her newly discovered feminine wiles to convince him that the twenty-year difference in their ages wasn't important. Six months after they met, they were married.

While he'd been alive, she'd thought of him as masterful and tenacious. This morning, she'd been shocked to discover the same traits had struck her as male chauvinistic and bullheaded. Yet Skip O'Malley was still the first man she'd ever loved.

She glanced at Cam, wondering if he knew where her thoughts had taken her. He was staring straight ahead, unaware she was watching him, and the look of sadness and frustration on his face made her chest tighten painfully. He was the man she loved *now*. The man who deserved her unqualified support. She reached out for his hand.

"I thought you were asleep."

"I just needed to collect myself."

She looked around, expecting to see the route to the Plantation. Instead they were in a woods that was bright with the vibrant yellows, oranges and reds of fall. On the way to Jessup, she hadn't even noticed the trees.

Now she tried to enjoy the display Cam was providing. It took several moments for Jo to realize where he was taking her.

"We're in Worthington Valley."

"Umm. I thought this might be a good place to unwind a little bit." He was dividing his attention between the rearview mirror and the road.

"What are you looking for?"

"A tail. I want to make sure that O'Malley wasn't right—that the junkyard crisis wasn't a setup to get us out in the open where we'll be vulnerable."

"I'm the one who's supposed to pay attention to stuff like that." Flushing slightly, Jo pushed herself erect and glanced over her shoulder. The road behind them was clear.

"You've got a lot on your mind."

"*Was* someone behind us? Is that why you picked this route?"

"I haven't spotted anybody, but I was being cautious." He sighed. "I probably should take you home where you'll be safe."

She caught the wistful note in his voice and tightened her hand over his. "We have to talk but there isn't much privacy at the house."

"I know."

"I think it's safe to stay away for a while. Remember that spot where we used to picnic? We could go there."

She watched caution and temptation war on his face. Temptation won. "If you're sure."

"Yes."

He seemed glad that she'd made the decision, but he didn't say anything more for several miles.

When he turned off the pavement onto a gravel road that led between neon orange maples and more subdued red oaks, she felt a surge of freedom. Several hundred yards later, the car came to a stop beside a shallow river that splashed over dark boulders.

They'd discovered this hideaway during the first year of their marriage when they'd gotten into the habit of knocking off work early on Friday and playing hooky. The memories made Jo smile as she looked around.

Cam unhooked his safety belt and slid his seat back so that he could stretch out his long legs. The pose looked relaxed, but she knew him too well to be fooled.

"Thanks for bringing me here," she murmured.

"I have my selfish reasons. I want to be alone with you."

Without touching him, she felt the terrible tension in his body, caught the look of uncertainty that flashed across his face. Just when he'd discovered why she'd really gone down to the warehouse, he'd been given a new reason to question her commitment to their marriage. His doubts tore at her more deeply than the pain of getting shot.

She unbuckled her seat belt and swung around to face him, her eyes seeking and holding his. "Cam, I love you very much. I can't stand the idea of anything pulling us apart."

"What about *him?*"

She touched his arm and felt his muscles tighten. "We left him back at the house. I don't want to drag him out here." Neither of them seemed willing to mention his name.

"Neither do I." He drew in a ragged breath, and she was afraid he was going to cut off the discussion. Then his face took on a resigned expression. "But I've got to know how you feel."

"Shocked. I'm having trouble coping."

"You married him. I assume you loved him." His gaze on her face was like a physical force.

She tried to put as much reassurance into her eyes as into her voice. "I was a different person then—younger, less sure of myself. You know about my background. He gave me a stability I'd never had before."

But Cam was like a hound that had picked up a blood trail. "So how do you compare us? Do you ever wish I was more like him?"

"No!"

"He's got insights I lack. Talents. Maybe right now you need him more than you do me."

"No! Cam, stop doing this to yourself—to me." She couldn't take any more of his pain—or hers. Scooting over the hump between the seats, she landed in his lap and cut off his startled exclamatión by covering his mouth with hers.

The contact was like a powerful electric circuit closing. They both gasped at the potency of the union. Then his lips began to move over hers—hungry, wild, demanding entrance.

She furnished it gladly, her whole body shuddering with pleasure as his tongue slipped into her mouth. The passion simmering between them for weeks rocketed out of control as they gave and received kiss after scorching kiss.

Yet mere kisses satisfied neither one of them for long. Without conscious thought, Jo shifted her position so that she was straddling his lap, her knees on either side of his legs, her body pressed intimately to his. His hips surged upward against her, and she smiled.

Shocking the very proper Cameron Randolph with her lack of inhibitions had been one of the great pleasures of their early marriage. But he'd taken the idea of

making love in a car parked in the woods very nicely.
With easy familiarity, his hands swept under her shirt,
unhooked her bra and pushed it out of the way. Then he
sought her breasts, cupping, kneading, shaping them to
his pleasure—and hers. When his fingers touched the
bullet scar, she froze and made a tiny noise in her
throat.

"Did I hurt you?" he asked urgently.

"No. It's just—"

Her heart pounded as he gently stroked the puckered
skin. Then, very slowly, he drew up her shirt, his eyes
locked with hers.

She'd imagined this moment—in a darkened bedroom, not in the sun-dappled woods. She held her
breath as he looked at her scar.

"It's ugly," she blurted.

"No, it's not. It's a reminder. Every time I touch it,
I'll remember what I almost lost."

"Oh, Cam."

As he pressed his lips to the scar, tears welled in her
eyes.

"I love you, Jo. I love every part of you."

His healing touch, his loving words reassured her, and
she began to enjoy the sensuality of his lips and tongue
caressing her. He moved his face back and forth against
her, breathing deeply, turning his head so that his
mouth could capture one hardened nipple.

The surge of sensation was so intense that she whim-
pered and rocked her hips against his.

A deep shudder of response racked his body. "I need
you."

"And I need you."

Jo raised her hips, and Cam skimmed down her sweatpants, along with her panties. She kicked them off and unzipped his jeans.

When she'd freed his hot, distended flesh, she caressed him lovingly, glorying in his hoarse cry of response and in her control of their lovemaking.

"I love you. Oh, God, I love you so much." She gasped as she moved to bring him inside her. The joining of their bodies was an affirmation of that love. Of everything right and good.

He said her name over and over as she began to move her hips in the erotic rhythm that they both knew so well. She wanted to make the wonderful sensations last. But there was no hope of slowing down. It was a sharp urgent coupling. A man and a woman professing their commitment in the most basic way. After denying themselves for so long, pleasure quickly built to an unendurable peak, and within moments they both cried out in joy and satisfaction.

Jo collapsed against her husband, her arms circling his neck, her head on his shoulder. She clung to him, murmuring her pleasure as his lips skimmed the side of her cheek.

"I needed that." She sighed.

"Oh, yeah?" He laughed. "Have I ever told you what a sexy little wood nymph you are?"

"Um-hum. But I'll never get tired of hearing it." She closed her eyes and snuggled into his warmth.

He held her for a long time, but finally they had to move. Jo grinned at him as she reached to retrieve her sweatpants, but his expression was sober.

She dressed, hoping he'd reach over and touch her again. Instead, after he'd buckled his pants, he got out of the car and walked down to the riverbank. Picking up a handful of stones, he began skipping them across the dark water. Except for the sound of the rocks hitting the surface of the river, silence hung in the air like an obscuring fog. Jo hesitated. His body language said he wanted to be alone. Yet she couldn't believe that. Quietly she came up beside him. "Cam?"

He tossed another stone.

"Talk to me."

"I managed to forget about him for a while."

"It was bad enough coping with an anonymous ghost. Finding out it was Skip was—" she struggled to express what she felt "—unnerving."

"I think it was more than that for you," he said in a gritty voice.

She felt the blood drain from her face as she pictured how she must have looked. "Cam, the day he died, we had a fight because I didn't want him to go out on that assignment. When I saw him standing in the lab, all I could think of was that the last emotion between us was anger."

"I'm sorry."

Did Cam understand? Or was he telling her he never would? "He came back because he thought I was in danger. Maybe we need him."

"Maybe he's lying. Maybe he came back to take you away from me."

"That's not true!"

"It's pretty clear he'd be thrilled if I were out of the picture. Which is exactly the way I feel about him."

Jo seized Cam's hands and held them in a death grip, wishing she knew how to handle this bizarre triangle.

"You were married to Skip O'Malley before you met me. You'd still be married to him if he hadn't gotten himself killed."

"Stop it. I'm married to you now. Heart and soul. When we made love, couldn't you tell how I feel about you, about us?"

"I thought so. Then I began picturing myself taking you home, taking you directly up to the bedroom and doing things right. Not quick and dirty in the front seat of a car."

"Quick and dirty was wonderful."

"But then I remembered that I can't make love to you in our bedroom because your late husband will be standing at the foot of the bed. Watching. Maybe even commenting on my performance."

"You're a lot better lover than he ever was," she admitted, then flushed.

"Yeah?"

"Cam, stop it! I'm not going to start comparing the two of you." She folded her arms across her chest. "I think it would be a big mistake to reassure you by saying stuff about him that's going to make me feel bad later. I did love him. But I was just a kid, and I was looking for a loving father as much as I was for a husband. He and I had a much different relationship from ours. He was a thirty-eight-year-old bachelor when we met, and he was set in his ways. I had to make myself fit into his life-style. I'm a different person now." She stopped, feeling guilty she'd gone so far, yet hoping she'd made Cam feel more secure about their marriage.

"I'm sorry," he muttered. "I can't help it. I'm jealous."

"Don't be! I'm going to feel the same lack of privacy when we get home. Remember, the whole thing's worse for me than it is for you."

"I doubt it."

"You've only got to cope with your feelings. I'm stuck between the two of you, and I don't know how to handle it."

Chapter Nine

"Jo, I don't want to make this harder for you."

"I know. But we're going to have to live with it for a while." She moved closer to him and circled his body with her arms. As they stood in the fall brilliance of the woods, hugging each other tightly, Jo let a seductive fantasy play through her mind. She and Cam could stop home long enough to pick up the tent and other equipment they'd need. Then they could check into one of the state's campgrounds. Nobody would find them. They'd be perfectly safe. And Skip would go back where he'd come from before she got any more involved with him.

It was Cam who finally broke the spell. "We have to get that film to Jason. Maybe the guy you were photographing is the one who shipped the car to the junkyard."

She nodded against his chest, feeling her world shrink. But she was determined to take as much control of her life as she could. "He might be. But we can go another route, too. Remember that visual identity software you put on my computer last year so I could help crime victims identify assailants?"

"Sure."

"You could work on a composite picture of the guy who was operating the wrecking equipment. Maybe he's got a rap sheet, and the police will have a lead on him."

They returned to the car, and Cam took the most direct route to the Plantation, scanning the road in back and in front of them as he approached their property. From the keypad in Jo's glove compartment, he accessed the security codes that opened the entrance gates. Usually he then made a quick check of the sentry system. Today after driving inside, he used the car's computer to query the sensor points around the grounds and in the house. All of them flashed a green light, indicating that no one was lying in wait inside.

As Jo watched him, she felt her stomach tighten in claustrophobic reaction. The only parts of the system she'd ever used after a few practice sessions with Cam was the mechanism that locked and unlocked the gate and opened the garage door. She supposed she was going to have to get in the habit of checking the sensors every time she came in. If Cam let her leave again. And who was he going to let inside now that he knew about the flower delivery? Probably even the gardener was going to need a special clearance.

"I guess it's lucky ghosts don't register on the equipment, otherwise we'd be getting some false positive readings," Cam muttered as he proceeded up the driveway.

"Skip would let us know if an intruder were here," Jo said.

Cam gave her a sharp look. "I'd rather trust my electronics, thanks." He pulled directly into the garage where he checked a more elaborate security readout. She saw him brace for some kind of assault as he unlocked the door. With an audible sigh, he stepped across the threshold.

She joined him in the silent hallway. No one was in the house, yet it was impossible to believe they were really alone. She almost called out Skip's name, but she stopped herself as she gave Cam a quick glance.

He made directly for her office and sat down at the desk where he picked up the phone and arranged for a courier from Randolph Security to get the film. Then he accessed the suspect identification program on the computer.

"Want a sandwich while you're working?" she asked.

"Are you sure you don't want to rest?"

"I'm hungry," she lied. "How about ham and cheese?"

"That sounds good," he said with false enthusiasm.

Jo left the room, feeling guilty that she needed to be alone for a while.

The kitchen was large and packed with the latest major appliances and gadgets, but she'd hardly been in it since she'd come back from the hospital. The thought of whipping up one of her famous country breakfasts had little appeal, but a couple of ham-and-cheese sandwiches weren't beyond her present capabilities. Maybe she could even manage some mugs of gourmet canned soup.

Revolving pantry shelves were concealed behind cabinet doors along one whole wall of the kitchen. On her way to get the soup, Jo switched on the radio built into the intercom system. Music from her favorite light-rock station immediately filled the kitchen. It was a Bob Seger oldie. "Still the Same." Not likely, Jo thought as she checked the labels on the cans. Split pea should go with the sandwiches.

The music stopped abruptly as if someone had switched from the radio to the intercom.

"Cam? Do you want anything?"

"It's not Cam. Aren't you going to tell me what happened?"

Jo jumped a foot in the air and dropped the can she was holding. It clunked on the ceramic tile. When she turned around, Skip was standing in the corner of the kitchen. Well, not exactly Skip. His image. The way it had appeared in the lab.

Taken completely by surprise, she gaped at him. "I— I thought you needed the power from Cam's equipment to... to materialize."

"Tom Swift has quite a setup here. After you left, I started nosing around and discovered I could draw a minimum amount of power from his backup batteries. Tell me what you found out at the junkyard and why you were gone so damn long."

The question was gruff, which was a good indication that Skip had been worried about her. She turned away from his image so he wouldn't see the bright color that stained her cheeks. Her side trip to Worthington Valley with Cam was none of Skip's business. And he wouldn't want to hear about it.

She wasn't up to any more emotional turmoil. Striving to keep things between them on a neutral level, she gave him a summary of what had transpired in Jessup.

Before she was finished, a voice interrupted from the doorway. "Am I invited to this debriefing?"

Jo jumped again. "Cam! I didn't hear you."

"I came to see if you were okay."

"I started making lunch, and Skip interrupted." She made an ineffective gesture with her hands.

"How interesting. So now we don't have to switch on the wave compressor to get the benefit of his wisdom. I wonder what other amazing new talents he's going to develop before this is over."

"Lots," Skip growled.

"We're going to make a composite picture of the man who was operating the compacting machinery. Do you want to help us?" Jo asked.

"How can he help? He wasn't there," Cam countered.

Jo shot him a pleading look, and he shut up. She started to leave the kitchen.

"You need to eat," Skip said.

"Why don't *you* fix her some lunch," Cam shot at him.

"I'll get it," Jo told him.

She slapped together some bread and ham and slathered them with mustard. She and Cam brought plates and soft drinks back to the office.

Skip hovered in the corner, no more than a dim shadow. If Jo hadn't known he was there, she might have missed him.

Cam sat down at the computer and they ate their sandwiches in silence—with a brief interruption when a messenger came from Randolph Security to pick up the film. After the driver left, Cam turned up the screen again. There was already a man's face partially sketched in—a man with long hair. It was as if Jo were seeing him lit from the back so the features were indistinct. But with just that much, a sensation of fear skittered through her.

"Have I made him nasty enough?" Cam asked as he saw her shiver.

Unable to take her gaze from the screen, Jo pulled up a chair and sat beside her husband, watching him make a series of changes on the lower part of the face. He wasn't getting it right. "He needs a more aggressive chin," she prompted.

Cam used the mouse to click on the chin area and give it more weight in the balance of the facial features. Pushing his chair back, he stared at the image. "That does look more like him. How did you know?"

She shrugged, feeling as if she were tiptoeing toward the edge of a precipice.

"You said you only saw him from the back."

"At the junkyard," she said hesitantly. It was hard to speak because her mouth had gone dry.

"You mean you may have seen him somewhere before? Has he been following you or something?"

"I haven't been anywhere." Her teeth worried her bottom lip. "Why don't you work on some of the other features?"

"Which?"

"The eyes."

Cam tried several different variations. Large wide eyes, deep-set eyes under hooded lids, small eyes close together.

"That!" Jo stopped him, feeling the hairs on the back of her neck move and stir. She knew as well as she knew her own name that she'd seen the emerging face before, but she didn't want to remember where.

"You've got a better visual sense than I do," Cam said as he sculpted the cheekbones.

"Who's supposed to be putting the picture together, you or her?" Skip's voice came from the corner, reminding Jo that he was still present.

"She seems to be contributing quite a bit," Cam retorted, but he started to work on the mouth by himself.

A tight knot coiled in her stomach as she stared at the result. The lips were narrow, but they weren't quite right. "Fuller bottom lip," she whispered, unable to staunch the details that were pouring into her brain. She wanted to stop making suggestions. Instead she said, "And try putting a scar right under his nose."

"That's right! A horizontal cut." Cam made the alteration.

Jo fidgeted in her chair and looked away from the screen, fixing on the books in the shelves above the desk. But she felt as if the man on the screen were staring at her malevolently. Against her will, her gaze was drawn back to him. It was as though she were seeing him clearly for the first time after a long absence. And she felt sheer terror gather like a storm cloud around her.

"Out with it," Skip said.

"Leave her alone," Cam shot in the direction of the ghost.

"No. He's right," she began in a low, stumbling voice. "When I was shot...I remember the gun. I didn't want to remember his face...but I think, um..." She understood now that the amnesia had been a protective mechanism to cut her off from memories too terrible to face. But she'd already broken the first barrier. Sitting in the car, she'd dredged up the image of the film. This afternoon she had gone even farther without realizing what was happening. Now all she had to do was say the words. So she pressed on. "The picture we're building up... He was the man who did it," she finished in a rush.

Cam stared from her to the screen and back again. "He's the guy who shot you? You're sure?"

"Now that we've got a reasonable likeness of his face, I feel as if it's etched into my brain with acid."

Blood pounded in her ears. Light-headed, she swayed sideways in her chair, grabbing ineffectively to catch herself. Instantly Cam was beside her. When his strong arms enfolded her, she turned to him mutely. Thankful that his body was between her and the screen, she buried her face against his chest. She didn't want to look at that face. Those eyes. Because it was like staring at death.

Cam murmured soft, reassuring words that she hardly understood, but she focused on the sound of his voice, struggling to block out fear.

"Jo?"

She nodded against his chest, making an effort to pull herself together. "It can't be a coincidence—the guy who shot me turning up at the junkyard."

"No," he agreed.

She sat up straighter and ran her fingers through her hair. "That day my car wouldn't start, so I had to take yours."

"Right."

"And they were after *your* equipment. Does that mean my Mustang was sabotaged so I'd have to take the Lexus?"

Cam stared at her. "That would mean someone came into the garage that morning. But there wasn't a record of a security breach."

"Maybe they got to it down at 43 Light Street. They could have done something that wouldn't cause problems until the next morning."

"I'd like to believe that," he said.

"I want to see if Dan Cassidy can give us a lead on the shooter," Jo said.

"I can give you a lead on him." The offer came from the corner of the room.

Both Jo and Cam jerked around. With her emotions roiling, she'd forgotten about Skip. But he had been there all the time.

"Who is he?" she asked.

"A hood named Frankie the Wrench who's supposed to be good at jobs requiring a mechanic. Last name's Waldon or something like that. Been in and out of the Patuxent Institution. Safecracking. Assault with a deadly weapon. Before that, he was a reform school graduate. Now they can get him for attempted murder, if they can catch him."

"Thanks." Jo didn't question the information, not when she knew Skip's phenomenal memory for cases. All at once it looked a lot more likely that they'd catch the man who'd shot her—and get to the bottom of the whole mystery.

"Remember my inactive files you stored upstairs in the attic? You'll find a folder on Frankie," he said.

"How do you know about the files?" Cam snapped.

"I've seen the boxes."

"Seen, not pawed through?"

"I can't affect objects in the material world."

Jo heard a note of frustration in his voice.

Cam didn't pause to examine the ghost's emotions. "Wait a minute. You pushed Jo back into the house when she tried to leave. And you hurled an energy bolt at me."

"Hurling energy's one thing. I'm made of energy, in case you haven't figured that out. Opening boxes is different."

"From slamming doors?"

"That was an emergency. But it just about cleared my clock."

"Too bad it didn't," Cam muttered. "You must be some kind of open system," he added.

"What?" Jo asked.

"Under the laws of thermodynamics—"

"Which are?" she prompted.

"The laws governing the conversion of energy from one form to another. An open system exchanges mass, heat and work with the surroundings—as opposed to a closed system that exchanges heat and work but not mass." He addressed Skip again. "What about walking through walls? Can you do that?"

"A crude way to put it, but the answer is yes."

"How?"

"I don't know *how*. I haven't memorized the laws of thermodynamics. I just *do* it. But I can't get the folder. You're going to have to do that."

IT TOOK LESS TIME than Jo might have imagined to locate the material, since the inactive files were in more or less alphabetical order. Skip had been right about Frankie's last name.

Excitement mixed with foreboding surged in her chest as she and Cam divided up twenty pages of detailed records on Frankie. Finally they were getting somewhere. But how close did she want to get to this guy again?

The records terminated ten years earlier when Frankie had been working for an auto-theft ring that Skip had helped break up. The last entry noted that he was in the Maryland State Penitentiary.

"It's a pretty cold trail," she muttered.

"Dan could tell us if there have been any subsequent arrests," Cam said.

"What about his contacts? Where did he hang out?" Skip asked.

Jo flipped several pages. "He was a boxer. Used to work out at a gym in Dundalk." She pulled the phone across the desk and dialed the number. It now belonged to a pizza parlor. A call to information established that there was no gym of the same name still operating.

Jo sighed. Cam gave her a critical look and then glanced at his watch. "Good Lord, it's almost eleven."

"No wonder the print is starting to blur."

"Let's knock it off for tonight."

Now that she was so close to confronting her fear, she wanted to press on. But she knew Cam was right. They weren't getting anywhere, and they were too exhausted to think of fresh approaches.

As they got up to go to bed, she glanced at Skip and then quickly away. *They* might need to sleep. He would be doing the same thing he had for weeks. She remembered all the times she had sensed his presence. Would he turn invisible and follow them up to the bedroom the way Cam had speculated?

Jo closed her eyes for a moment, glad that she and Cam were both too tired to do anything more than sleep. But that was tonight. What about all the other nights they were going to lie beside each other, craving intimacy but knowing they might be observed? She had no idea how they were going to manage, no idea how their marriage was going to survive that kind of strain.

AT SEVEN IN THE MORNING, after a restless night, Jo sat bolt upright in bed. "I wonder if the mother's still alive."

"What?" Cam mumbled.

"I remember something in the file about Frankie's mother. She had an unusual name. If she's still in Baltimore, maybe we can get in touch with her."

"She's not going to tell you anything," Cam answered.

"She might—with the right approach." Skip's voice pierced the sanctity of their bedroom, confirming Jo's worst fears about their privacy.

Cam sat up and swore. "Have you been skulking around in here all night?"

The ghost was leaning against the bureau. "No. I heard you talking. I've been waiting for you to wake up."

"Why don't we get dressed, and you can meet us downstairs," Jo said. To her relief, Skip quickly agreed, as if he realized he'd overstepped the bounds of propriety.

Twenty minutes later they reassembled in the den. The flesh-and-blood members of the trio had coffee and the blueberry muffins that Jo kept in the freezer.

"What approach were you thinking about, Skip?" Jo asked.

"First see if you can get her number from information."

There was a number listed for a Demetra Waldon, and the name was unusual enough that it was probably the right one.

Jo started to dial again.

"Let me make the call," Skip said.

"You?" Cam asked.

Jo, who'd often witnessed Skip O'Malley as consummate con artist, set the receiver on the desk as he directed.

The buttons on the phone didn't move, but they could hear the circuits clicking.

"Hello." The woman's voice that answered was more robust than Jo had expected.

"Is this Mrs. Waldon?" Skip asked, his voice coming to them through the phone's speaker.

"This is her daughter, Mrs. Keiser."

"I'm trying to get in touch with Frank Waldon."

The woman turned cautious. "Why?"

"This is ABC Pawn Shop. Mr. Waldon left some merchandise with us that's reaching the end of its redemption period."

"You mean the silver place settings the bum took from my mother a couple of months ago? Is that what he did with it?"

"Well, of course, we have no knowledge of how the items were obtained. But I *am* referring to silver flatware."

"That bastard! Ma worked and slaved all her life for her kids, and this is how he rewards her."

"If the merchandise was not Mr. Waldon's to pawn, we would be willing to return it to the owner. But we would need proof of ownership."

"Thanks a lot. But I can't *prove* it's her stuff. She inherited it from my grandmother."

"Perhaps you could persuade your brother to give you the original ticket."

"Fat chance." The woman hung up.

Puzzled and disappointed that Skip hadn't thought of a more effective approach, Jo also replaced the receiver.

"Now what?" Cam asked.

"Frankie's number is 555-7157," Skip informed him. "But he's not answering the phone."

"How do you know all that?" Cam demanded.

"I stayed on the line after you disconnected." As he spoke, he materialized in the corner of the room again. "That's the number his sister dialed right after talking with me. I presume Frankie is the most likely candidate."

"You knew you could do that?" Jo asked.

"I've practiced on some of your phone calls."

"That's an invasion of privacy!" Cam objected.

"You could say that about almost everything a private eye does."

Cam swung his attention to Jo, who looked down at her hands. She wouldn't have put it quite that bluntly, but she supposed it was an accurate description.

"Do you have a cross-reference phone directory at home?" Skip asked Jo.

"My old one. In the bottom left desk drawer." She pulled it out and looked up the number Mrs. Keiser had dialed. It was at an address on High Street. After writing it down, she stared thoughtfully at the piece of paper.

"I know that look," Skip said. "What's wrong?"

"I was just thinking."

"About?"

"Maybe I'm missing something, but why did you let Frankie's sister think he had a pawn ticket for their mother's silver?"

"So she'd call him. It worked, didn't it?"

"Yes, but *he* knows he doesn't have the ticket. When she talks to him, why won't he suspect something funny's going on?"

"Maybe he *did* pawn the silver!"

"We don't know for sure."

For several seconds there was dead silence from the ghost.

Jo saw that Cam was about to say something derogatory and clamped her hand around his wrist. Jumping on Skip now wasn't going to help the situation. "You haven't done this kind of work in a long time," she said.

Skip cursed self-deprecatingly. "That's no excuse. Jo, I may have blown this for you."

"Not if Cam and I get to Frankie's house before his sister reaches him." The suggestion popped out before she had time to think it through. Taking charge was always her natural response. Still she felt fear prickle along her nerve endings when she thought about getting anywhere near Frankie. Which was why she *had* to.

"What do you mean, Cam and you? The guy tried to kill you. You're going to let the police go in and get him."

"You wouldn't have done it that way," she reminded him, surprised at how steady her voice sounded.

"Right." He snorted. "I liked taking chances. Look where it got me."

Jo heard the pain in his voice. Her heart squeezed, and she wanted to reach out and hug him, like a mother comforting a child who'd slipped and skinned his knee. It was a complete reversal of roles, as disorienting as anything that had happened since he'd followed her back to earth.

"I'll call Dan and get him to issue a search warrant," Cam said.

Jo shook her head. "That won't work. All we have is a composite picture, a ghost's word that it's of someone named Frankie the Wrench and my suspicion that he's the one who shot me. But that's not enough for a search warrant. I'd have to identify him in a lineup first. And what if I did? He's obviously working for someone with clout, someone with a good lawyer who'll have him out of jail before we can blink."

Skip sighed. "You're right."

"So now we have the perfect opportunity to do some investigating while he's not home."

"It's too dangerous. He could come back at any time," Cam said.

She reached out to take his hand, gripping his fingers tightly. "Cam, just looking at his picture on the computer screen yesterday terrified me. I didn't like that feeling. He took something important away from me, and now I have an opportunity to get it back. Do you understand what that means to me?" She looked at him pleadingly, begging silently for him to understand.

"Jo, your reaction is perfectly understandable. But putting you in danger isn't part of *my* agenda."

Her eyes turned fierce as they drilled into him, and she went on as if she hadn't heard him. "Here's how we'll do it. You'll stay outside and keep watch. Since I'm the one who knows how to search, I'll go in, and we'll keep in touch by walkie-talkie. If he shows up, you can let me know, and I'll get out. It's going to be perfectly safe."

"No," man and ghost said at the same time.

"Use your friend Jason instead of Jo," Skip added.

"He's out on a job."

"We're wasting time," Jo said. "In fact, we may already be too late. He could have skipped town as soon as he escaped from the junkyard, and that's why he's not at home."

"Then there's no rush," Cam said.

"Or we may get there just in the nick of time," Jo countered. "Please, if I don't do this I won't be able to face myself."

She could see Cam still didn't like it. But finally he nodded tightly.

CAM LOOKED at the narrow streets of Little Italy, a neighborhood of row homes and restaurants sandwiched between Fell's Point and the Inner Harbor. He didn't like being here one damn bit, especially at nine-thirty in the morning when most people had left for work. He'd sworn he was going to protect Jo, so what in blazes were they doing on an expedition to break into a killer's house? More than once, he'd almost turned around and driven his wife back home where she'd be a lot safer. Then he'd taken another look at the fierce expression on her face. Frankie the Wrench had almost killed her. Even though she'd survived, he destroyed something inside her. Something she thought she couldn't get back unless she proved she wasn't afraid of the slime. On a gut level, he understood what she was going through—since it was so close to his own feeling of self-doubt. So he'd agreed to ride shotgun on a mission to hell.

He heard the stress in Jo's voice as she gave curt directions to Frankie's house.

"You can park in this alley. It's only about half a block from his address."

He sighed. Little Italy was notorious for its lack of parking spaces. But Jo had rented a room in the area when she'd first come from western Maryland to Baltimore, so she knew the locale well. Reaching in the back seat, she grabbed the walkie-talkies.

After cutting the engine, he grimly checked the units. "I still don't like this setup. *You* be the lookout. *I'll* go inside."

"You're more likely to miss something."

"Right. You were trained by the famous Skip O'Malley."

"Cam, we're wasting time." She didn't say any more, but her eyes begged him to let her get it over with.

"You're not going in there until I make sure Frankie's not home."

"How?"

"Knock on the door."

"And if he answers?"

"I'll tell him I'm selling encyclopedias."

JO WAITED TENSELY across the street while Cam rang the bell several times. Worrying about him gave her a little taste of what he must be feeling about this whole operation.

The knot in her stomach loosened just a little when it appeared that no one was home. On the other hand, Frankie might be crouched below the window frame with a revolver in his hand. She pressed her lips together. She wasn't going to mention that possibility to her husband. Instead she felt for the gun she'd tucked in the waistband of her slacks—the gun she also hadn't mentioned to Cam because she knew it would make him reevaluate letting her go inside alone.

They regrouped by the back door, where she coolly pulled on a pair of rubber gloves and used her lock-picking tools on the dead bolt. The door opened, and she stared into the dimly lit interior. She didn't have to do this by herself. Cam could come inside, too. Then she shook her head. It would be worse if Frankie came home and they were both taken by surprise. Before Cam could hold her back, she stepped across the threshold and closed the door. Almost immediately the walkie-talkie sprang into life.

"You okay?"

"Cam, I'm fine." She put as much conviction as she could into her voice, glad he couldn't feel the vibration of her heart through her shirt. It was pounding so hard, she had to stop for a minute and steady herself. Ears straining, she listened for any sign that the house might be occupied. All she could hear was the refrigerator whining in the corner.

Frankie had closed all the blinds, which made it easier to move around inside without being seen. Pulling off the cap covering her red curls, she switched on a penlight and made a quick search of the kitchen—which was easy to scope out, since the cabinets were practically empty and the refrigerator was stocked only with beer. Then the rest of the house loomed as dangerous unknown territory.

Cautiously she approached the living room, but found nothing more interesting than the remains of fast-food dinners on the dirty rug and clusters of empty beer bottles on the scarred coffee table. The food smelled pretty rotten, as if it had been sitting around moldering for days. Then Jo realized the odor wasn't coming from the bags and plastic containers. It was wafting in from the little room at the very front of the house. Her fingers clamped down on the walkie-talkie in her hand as she tiptoed closer. Craning her neck around the corner, she spotted a shoe lying on the floor. Well, not just a shoe. It was attached to a trouser-covered leg.

She screamed.

Chapter Ten

"Jo, what is it?" Cam charged into the room.

"He's dead—or he took care of someone else and cleared out." See pointed to the foot.

"Stay here."

It wasn't the kind of order she usually followed. Feeling queasy, she let Cam do the honors.

He was back in less than a minute, his expression grim. "It's the man who was operating the equipment. I'd say he was strangled."

"I'd say we'd better get out of here."

"We have to report a murder to the police."

"Yeah, but do you really want to explain how we broke in and found the body?"

"Good point."

Amazed that she could focus on covering their tracks, Jo looked at her husband's bare hand. "They're going to go over this place with a fine-tooth comb. Did you touch anything?"

"Just the door and the knob."

"Wipe them off." Her own hands had turned clammy inside the rubber gloves. "I want to have a look at Frankie's face before we leave."

"No, you don't."

She swallowed hard. "I only saw that composite sketch. I have to make sure he's really the man who shot me."

She started toward the protruding foot. Cam grabbed her hand. Gripping him tightly, she stepped through the doorway and confronted the body. Frankie was lying on his back. His face was splotchy red. His eyes bugged out, and his neck was a massive bruise where a cord had bitten into his flesh, strangling him. He looked like the victim of a gangland execution.

"Cam, have you been threatened by the mob? Is that who's after you?"

"Not that I know of, but maybe Jason ought to dig a little deeper into the warehouse owner's connections."

Jo nodded before turning her attention back to the dead man. The identification took only a moment. Although his features were distorted, he was definitely the one who had shot her. But she wasn't going to get a chance to ask him any questions.

"Someone wanted to make damn sure he didn't tell what he knows," she murmured as she turned her face into Cam's shoulder.

With his arm protectively around her, he steered her back into the living room. "Or they may have decided he was expendable because he was spotted at the junkyard."

"I hope nobody spotted *us* when we came in," Jo murmured as they made their way back to the kitchen.

Thrusting her behind him, Cam opened the door and took several seconds to make sure the coast was clear. Then, after wiping the surfaces he'd touched, he motioned for her to follow. She put on her cap and pulled the visor low over her face. Cam folded up his collar and ducked his head. Trying to look as if they belonged in the neighborhood on a weekday morning, they returned to the car.

Jo directed him to a pay phone on Broadway where he made an anonymous call to the police.

A tremendous feeling of relief swept over her as they vacated the area. It was finally sinking in that the man who'd shot her was dead, and there was nothing else he could do to her. "I guess we report the incident at the junkyard to Dan and tell him you did a composite picture of the guy operating the crushing equipment. I was helping you and thought he was the shooter who took me out. If we fax him the picture, he may connect it with the new arrival in the morgue."

"Can't we give him Frankie's name?"

She had already gone through that silent debate. "Dan will know I wouldn't pass up the opportunity to collect some evidence."

"Of course not," he said evenly.

He saw her slide him a questioning glance and almost made another comment about her knee-jerk P.I. responses. But he wasn't up to starting another argument.

"I had to prove I wasn't wimping out."

Even though he understood why they'd gone to Frankie's, he couldn't stop himself from shooting back. "Are you going to have to *keep* proving it?" He could hear the tone of his voice putting a wall between them.

She turned away from him as if she were absorbed in the scenery passing outside the window. "I don't know."

He wanted to explain that since they'd burglarized a criminal's apartment and stumbled over a dead body, he had an even firmer conviction that detective work wasn't an ideal career choice for his wife.

He wanted to make her understand how much he loved her and how incomplete his life had been before they'd met. He wanted to pour out how devastated he'd be if he lost her. But he simply couldn't expose any more of his insecurities than he'd already laid bare. So they drove in silence while he made plans for how he was going to keep her safe—despite herself.

After several miles, he realized from her regular breathing that she'd fallen asleep after the morning's exertions.

Good. That would make things easier.

CAM LEFT JO SLEEPING in the car and slipped into the house. The minute he stepped into the hall, a semi-transparent image of Skip O'Malley confronted him like a spook in a cut-rate horror movie.

"What happened to Jo?"

"She's sleeping in the car."

"Bring her in," the ghost commanded.

"No. She's exhausted, and there are some things I need to do before she wakes up."

"Are you going to tell me what you found at Frankie's?"

"His body."

Skip swore.

"So now Jo's proved her courage, and I can do what I should have done a couple of days ago."

"What?"

Deliberately he turned away and strode toward the den.

But evading the ghost wasn't that simple. Skip winked into existence in the middle of the room. "Answer me, you bastard."

Cam came back with an equally insulting curse. "I don't have to be polite to you when Jo's not around. Buzz off, and let me take care of my own business."

Static electricity crackled around the spectral image, a visible manifestation of his anger. "Jo's the only thing stopping me from zapping you."

"Yeah? Well, I think you're impotent without my wave compressor."

He turned his back on the visual display, half expecting to feel another deadly arrow pierce his flesh. Baiting O'Malley was pretty stupid. He switched on his voice-encryption equipment and dialed Jason's extension at Randolph Security.

"I've developed that roll of film," Jason said as soon as he recognized Cam's voice. "It's shots of a guy lurking around the warehouse. I've sent copies to the FBI to try and get a make on him."

Cam told Jason about Frankie. "Since the dead man was local talent, maybe this other guy is, too. So send the package to the Baltimore police." He thought for a moment. "And try that new photo-enhancement program we bought. You might get lucky and find some distinguishing details that could give us a lead."

"Good idea. Anything else?"

He could feel Skip's gaze burning into the back of his neck. It gave him enormous satisfaction to ignore the ghost.

"There is one more thing," he told Jason. "I want Jo out of here until we find out who's after the wave compressor and put the son of a bitch away."

"You're right. We're better off if she's not in the thick of things. Where's she going? To visit friends out of town?"

He half expected Skip to jump in with suggestions, but the specter remained silent. "We can't be predictable. Since Mr. X seems to be one step ahead of us every time we make a move, we've got to stash Jo someplace absolutely secure. Pick a couple of locations and make arrangements. We'll choose the actual destination when we get to the airport."

"Do you want to send Noel with her?"

"I'd appreciate it. Jason, thanks for everything."

"I know what you're going through."

The feeling of being observed had intensified. Hanging up, Cam raised his head to confront O'Malley. Instead, his gaze collided with Jo's. She took a step into the room; her eyes burned with green fire.

"What do you think you're doing?" she demanded.

"I thought you were asleep."

"Unfortunately for you, I woke up in the middle of your macho strategy session."

"Getting you out of harm's way is the only smart thing to do. We're not having any more adventures like our little visit to Frankie's."

"But that doesn't mean I have to leave town."

"Yes, it does. Jo, try to understand. Your safety is nonnegotiable. Remember we were talking about Art Nugent a few days ago?"

"That was before we knew the ghost was Skip."

"Don't you understand how I felt when Art took you away from me? I almost went out of my mind. I swore I'd never let anything like that happen again."

Her face contorted, but she didn't give in. "This is different. I was in a public place. The reception hall for Abby's wedding. And Art had it all planned."

"Yeah? Well, we don't know about the plans of whoever's after the wave compressor. The only thing we know is that he's willing to terrorize and kill to get what he wants. Jo, don't you see, as long as I'm torn up with worry about you, I can't concentrate on solving this problem. So I want you to go upstairs and pack a couple of suitcases. Tomorrow you and Noel are leaving on a short vacation. By the time you get back, everything's going to be resolved."

Jo stood with her hands on her hips. "Cam, that's not the solution. I'm a grown woman. You can't make decisions for me."

"In this case, I have to. You're letting your emotions override your common sense. You're taking risks that are driving me up the wall."

"I know what I'm doing! And you need my investigative skills to crack this case."

"They didn't save you from Art. Or down at the warehouse." He sighed. "But if I need a detective's insights, I have Skip O'Malley."

The ghost's image became sharper. "That's right."

Jo whirled toward him. "Whose side are you on?"

"Yours."

"Then why are you going along with him?"

"Because somebody wants to get to Cam. They've already tried to use you, and there's no reason they won't do it again."

Jo's angry gaze swung from man to ghost and back again, settling on the more solid of the pair. "It looks like you two have my life all figured out."

Cam tried to interrupt, but she was too wound up to listen.

"You don't need me." Her eyes—wounded and defiant—drilled into Cam's. "Especially you. I've been trying my damnedest to make this marriage work. Now you're making me wonder if it's worth the effort." Before he could reply, she turned and marched toward the door.

Jo managed to hold back the tears burning her eyes until she'd stepped outside the French doors that led to the garden. Her first thought was to get back into the Mustang, drive to her office at 43 Light Street and lock the door behind her. At least down there she could make her own decisions. But Safety Officer Randolph would have a heart attack if she tried to leave the grounds, and he'd doubtlessly change the combination on the gate if he heard the car start up in the garage.

The tears started to flow in earnest down her cheeks. Cam had taken her to Frankie's, and she'd thought he understood how she felt. But he'd just been humoring her until he could think of how to get her out of the way.

It wasn't fair! The only reason she'd gotten into this mess was because she'd been trying every way she could to protect him. And her P.I. background could still make the difference in how this whole thing shook out. But the blind fool couldn't see it. All he could think about was that he didn't like his wife being a private detective, and he wasn't going to let her do anything more dangerous than going after deadbeat dads for child support. No, on second thought, *that* was probably too heavy for him.

In a fog of anger and frustration, she stumbled down the path, oblivious to the garden and hardly aware of where she was going until the summerhouse loomed in front of her. It was a tiny Victorian cottage designed like one of the houses in a church Christmas display that had fascinated her as a child. One of the few extravagances she'd indulged herself in with Cam's money was having a room-size replica built in the garden. Sometimes she came here when she had problems to work out. Sometimes she just came to relax and enjoy the solitude.

Today she rushed inside and headed straight for the elaborate wicker rocking chair by the wood stove. Huddling in the dim light, she rocked back and forth in misery. Deep down a little part of her knew she wasn't being fair, that she should never have flung that threat at Cam. But he'd started making decisions without asking what she wanted to do. And he wouldn't even listen to her arguments. He was treating her like his property instead of his wife. It was one more blow in a long series of frustrating recent events. The last straw. And she was so angry and off-balance that she didn't know what to do.

THE MOMENT JO LEFT, Cam leapt up from the desk and followed her toward the door, his heart pounding. He intended to rush outside, grab her by the shoulders and make her explain that crack about their marriage. Or at least keep her from leaving. Then he saw her hesitate at the edge of the patio. When she started down one of the paths onto the grounds, the tension in his chest let up a notch. As she'd charged out of the room, he'd pictured her heading for the garage. But the only place she could be going was the summerhouse he'd built for her down in the garden.

He hesitated. Was it safe to let her go so far from the house? It better be. The estate was as secure as Fort Knox, and if he thought he had a chance of keeping Jo here he wouldn't be thinking about sending her away. But the past two days had set his teeth on edge. First Jo had tried to sneak out to the junkyard when she could have been walking into a trap. Then she'd come up with plans for breaking into a killer's house. And he knew that the next time a dangerous mission came up, she'd be right in the thick of it—unless he got her out of harm's way.

"She probably didn't mean it," the ghost broke into his thoughts.

"Oh, yeah?" Cam whirled to confront the specter on the other side of the desk.

"Red flies off the handle when she's mad."

"Not with me."

"She'll calm down in a—"

Before the ghost could finish, Cam stomped out of the room. The last thing he needed was O'Malley's advice on how to deal with his wife.

A SHADOW FELL across the room.

"Cam?"

"No."

Jo looked up from the rocking chair where she huddled with her arms folded tightly across her chest. It wasn't Cam standing over her. It was one of the men from the gardening service, dressed in his familiar blue uniform.

"Don't move."

There was nothing familiar about the rough way he spoke to her or the threatening way he blocked the door.

She blinked, struggling to make sense of what was happening. All at once it registered that he wasn't holding a trowel in his hand. It was a gun—an odd-looking gun—and it was pointed at her chest. His face was determined, and his eyes darted from side to side, as if he were as unnerved by this unlikely encounter as she.

Somehow she kept from gasping. Somehow she held her voice steady. "What do you want?" Oh, God. What had she gotten herself into? She stole a quick look at her watch. It was one in the afternoon. She'd been here for a little over an hour.

"Where's Randolph?"

"I don't know." At least he'd given her an important piece of information. Two pieces. He hadn't already done something to Cam, and he didn't know where he was.

"Your name's Monroe," she said.

He'd been on the job for several months, and he'd always been quiet and deferential. Now he growled a curse. "Shut your mouth and get up. We're going up to the house."

"Do you want money?" she asked, hoping against hope it was that simple.

"I said, shut up." Monroe flicked the wrist of his gun hand, and she stood, locking her knees to keep from swaying.

God, what was the best thing to do? Where was Cam? Could she get away? Warn him?

"Move!" He stepped aside so she could exit.

She began walking toward the house, her eyes scanning the path, every cell in her body aware of the man with the gun who was right behind her.

EVERY MINUTE Jo was out of his sight was an agony for Cam. But there was no use going to her until he'd thought of an argument that would make her see his point of view. She'd just look at him with those wounded eyes that made him feel as if razor wire were twisting in his gut. So he'd been pacing back and forth, trying to control his fears and thanking the Lord that at least O'Malley was leaving him alone.

He had gone into the kitchen to get a drink of water to moisten his dry mouth when the intercom crackled.

"Randolph!" O'Malley's voice was a low hiss.

"Don't tell me you're playing with the speaker system now," he growled.

"Pay attention to me. One of your gardeners is marching Jo up the path. She's walking like she's got a gun at her back."

The water glass clanked onto the counter. "What?"

"Either they're heading for the house or the van parked in the driveway."

Cam swore. "How—?"

O'Malley cut him off. "I can see them from the upstairs window."

Cam charged down the hall to get the gun Jo kept in her desk drawer. It wasn't there.

"She took it with her to Frankie's. She's got a spare in the top of the closet," the ghost barked.

"Thanks."

The specter kept talking as Cam made for a back window. "The truck pulled up while you were in the kitchen."

"The gardeners don't usually come two days in a row."

"Yeah, so I was curious. There are two of them. I didn't see where the other one went."

"Great! Where are Jo and the gunman now?"

"About fifty yards from the house."

Cam moved the curtains aside with the barrel of the gun. He couldn't see anyone in the garden, but he assumed O'Malley wasn't playing an insane practical joke.

JO PICTURED THE WEAPON aimed at her back. It didn't have a regular barrel. In fact, it looked more like a needle.

A tranquilizer gun! If he shot her, she'd only go to sleep. Unless he was using poison darts. But why do something so strange? So it would look as though she'd died of a heart attack instead of a bullet wound, her nimble mind provided an instant answer.

There was a bend in the path a few yards farther on—and a boulder that might serve as a shield. He wouldn't be expecting her to try to get away. Perhaps she could duck and roll behind the barrier.

She sifted through the possibilities while she moved up the path as slowly as she dared, alert for any sign of Cam.

"Can't you walk any faster?" Monroe snapped.

"I'm recovering from having a bullet dug out of my lung."

"You were running around like you felt pretty well this morning."

She cringed. My God. Did he know she and Cam had been to Frankie's? If he'd been supplied with information on that, then they'd been followed this morning. A sick feeling welled up in her throat. She'd been angry at Cam for being overprotective, and he'd been right.

Her anxiety increased as they moved up the hill. She could see the ground floor of the house. Her eyes flicked between the front door and the boulder that was now only a yard in front of her.

She'd have to make a decision in the next few seconds.

CAM TOOK PRECIOUS SECONDS to reset the access codes on the alarm system so the gate wouldn't open when the truck tried to leave the property. Then he sprinted down the hall to the garage.

"Where's Jo now?" he asked O'Malley.

"Near the top of the path. I can't tell which way they're going."

"If he's planning to load her in the van, I'll take him by surprise. If he brings her in the house, you put him out of commission." Cam's heart was pounding as he let himself out through the side door. Although he'd been condescending when Jo had dragged him to the firing range, he'd proved to be a pretty good shot. But the man moving up the path wasn't a paper target. And he had a gun trained on Jo.

He'd never thought he'd miss the sound of O'Malley's voice. But as soon as he slipped out the door, he knew he was on his own.

He edged to the end of the garage wall and peered around the corner. He could see them!

Jo was in the lead, her face drawn. The man was behind her. He said something Cam couldn't hear, and she veered toward the truck. Which meant that they'd both have their backs to him in another minute. Could he risk a shot? Could he shoot a man in the back, even if he had a gun trained on Jo?

What if he yelled out a warning to drop the gun? The man would turn, and Jo would roll to the ground—he hoped. Stepping out into the open, he moved closer.

''Freeze!''

The order didn't come from Cam; it came from another man who had glided from behind the gazebo, a weapon in his hand.

JO HEARD THE SHOUTED order. So did the man behind her. As he whirled around, she leapt away from him and threw herself at the boulder. But a sharp, stinging pain in her shoulder made her gasp. Her fingers closed around a metal shaft, and she pulled it out of her flesh.

Then she was staring stupidly at a small dart in her hand. Her vision swam, and she tried to blink away the gathering fog. Instead she toppled to her side.

''Jo!''

That was Cam. Cam's voice. Very far away.

She wanted so much to go to him, but she couldn't move. Couldn't see. Couldn't draw a full breath into her lungs.

Panic rose like a silent scream in her throat. Then blackness swallowed her up.

Chapter Eleven

A voice roared in his ears. The same words over and over. But he couldn't make his mind focus.

"Randolph. Damn you. Wake up. You've got to get Jo."

Jo. Her name brought a terrible sense of urgency. Doggedly he fought his way toward consciousness.

The first thing he became aware of was that he was lying on a hard, prickly surface. Then he realized a voice was calling him—had been calling him for a long time. Only he'd made it part of a dream.

His eyes blinked open. He was outside. On the grass, and he couldn't see very clearly. Fumbling over the ground, he found his glasses and put them on. He rolled to his back and stared up at the sky. Clouds had gathered while he'd slept, obscuring the sun.

His mouth tasted as though he'd gargled with battery acid, and his temples pounded. A gun was lying beside him on the grass.

He picked it up, hefting its weight in his hand.

A gun?

Memory came back in bits and pieces, like a patchwork quilt with some of the squares missing.

Jo. On the path. The man in back of her. Another man coming around the corner with a weapon in his hand.

His eyes flicked to the spot where the gardening service van had been. It was gone.

Jo was gone.

"Randolph."

He struggled to a sitting position, and a wave of dizziness threatened to sweep away consciousness. When his head stopped spinning, he looked toward the house.

"Can you walk?" The question came through the open garage door. It was O'Malley broadcasting at top volume through the intercom system.

Cam pushed himself up, swayed on shaky legs and staggered toward the house. The effort was more than he could maintain. Sweat beaded on his forehead. Panting, he caught himself on the doorframe. "How long have I been out?"

"Four hours and twenty-two minutes," O'Malley answered.

"Oh, Lord."

"It would have been longer if I hadn't kept at you. I guess you're feeling pretty punk."

"Yeah."

"After they shot you with the tranq gun, they loaded Jo in the van and left. She was unconscious, too."

He swore. "What about the gate? Didn't that stop them?"

"They didn't come back here."

Blackness threatened to claim him again. But he would not pass out. *He would not!* Teeth clamped together, Cam made it into the house to the control console for the security system. The alternate codes were still set. Not daring to hope for anything good, he brought up a television picture of the gate. When he focused in on the locking mechanism, he swore. It had been sliced in half with a blow torch or some sort of similar equipment.

Now he knew the worst. Jo was gone.

Kidnapped.

He'd sworn he'd never let anything like that happen again. He'd made plans to keep her safe. But they were too little and too late. He smugly thought this estate was safe. He'd been damn wrong. The effort to stay on his feet became too much. He sat down heavily on the steps.

"Don't just sit there," O'Malley shouted.

"Shut up." Anger and frustration seethed inside his chest. There was no focus for his wrath besides the ghost of Skip O'Malley. "If you weren't here, none of this would have happened."

"What the hell do you mean? Your wife's gone because some bozo is out to steal your latest invention."

"Oh, yeah. Well, we don't know for sure there's any connection. All we know is that if you weren't lurking in every room spying on us, Jo and I would be communicating with each other, and she wouldn't have stomped out of the door. She would have been with me. And when the gardener came into the house, he would have had to kill me first to get his hands on her."

There were several seconds of utter and absolute silence, as if O'Malley had no idea how to reply to such a self-serving outburst, even if it had a grain of truth.

"For God's sake, you hurled a thunderbolt at me down in the lab," Cam continued. "You didn't do a damn thing to stop the kidnappers."

"The thugs weren't in the house where I can be effective. Even if they had been, I need energy to generate fireworks. You carefully turned off your equipment last night, so I didn't have a power source.''

Cam closed his eyes and dug his fingers into the carpet fibers. Somehow he found the strength to speak reasonably. "Slashing at you isn't going to get Jo back."

Skip sighed. "We're both upset."

"Yeah." Cam pushed himself off the steps and started for the office, intending to call the police. Before he reached the phone, he realized involving the authorities could jeopardize Jo. He'd better find out what the kidnappers were after and how they wanted him to proceed before he called anyone besides Jason.

DEGREE BY ACHING DEGREE, Jo became aware of her surroundings. She was lying on a comfortable bed, dressed in sweatpants and a shirt. Cautiously she opened her eyes and tried to sit up, but a wave of dizziness and nausea threatened to overwhelm her, and she slumped against the pillow.

"Cam?"

When he didn't answer, she opened her eyes again. Her vision swam in and out of focus as she looked around the small room, cataloging an elegant brass bed, cream-colored walls, long mint green drapes. She was sure she'd never been in this place before. Trying to control her panic, she moved to the window. When she pulled back the curtains, she gasped. There was nothing behind the fabric except a blank wall. A cold sweat broke out on her forehead as she staggered to the door. She turned the knob, but it was locked from the outside.

"Is someone there?"

No one answered. In frustration, she pounded against the wood, but there was no response. And she didn't have the energy to keep banging. Another door led to a small bathroom. With shaky hands, she splashed cold water on her face, trying to clear the foggy confusion from her brain. Her bloodshot gaze in the mirror made her cringe. Her face was washed out, as pale as a bed sheet.

She leaned against the sink, forcing her mind to divulge what had happened. This morning. The man with the tranquilizer gun. The stinging pain in her shoulder; the dart in her hand. Then nothing. Someone had put her to sleep and brought her *here*.

But where was she? Where was Cam? She turned back to the bedroom, eyeing the hand-stitched quilt, plush carpet and the solid oak dresser. The place had the appearance of an expensive hotel—but with blank walls instead of windows, and doors that locked from the outside.

She was still searching for clues when an electronically distorted voice made her jump.

"Ms. O'Malley, I see that you are getting your bearings."

"Who are you?" Jo frantically scanned the room. She could see no speaker, although the sound seemed to be coming from near the ceiling.

The voice didn't answer.

"What do you want?" she demanded. Did he have a hidden camera, as well as a sound system, she wondered, clenching her fists at her side.

"I think it's time to stop playing games and tell me what's going on," she said with as much defiance as she could muster.

"How would you like to talk to your husband?"

"Cam is here, too?" Her heart leapt at the thought, then sunk as she realized the implications.

"No, but you're going to tell him how splendidly you're getting on."

"And if I don't?" She waited for his next words, ready to focus on his voice as much as what he was saying. He was trying to hide his accent with the electronic distortion. But she knew he wasn't American.

"The first thing you'd better learn, lass, is to do as you're told while you're here," the voice answered with an icy precision that sent a cold tremor down her spine.

"THE BEST YOU CAN hope for is that the kidnappers know how rich you are and want money," Skip advised, as if he'd read Cam's mind.

"Yeah," he muttered as he reached for the phone.

"Are you calling your buddy Jason?"

"Right."

"Assume the phone line's tapped. Tell him it's important, but don't give anything away until he gets here. And you might want to pull his wife in on this. She and Jo are friends. She might know something we don't."

"I think I'm smart enough to figure all that out," Cam snapped. "When they get here, keep your mouth shut."

"I was planning on it. I'm smart enough to know they'd spend the first hour and a half asking me questions. But I'll be listening."

Jason must have caught the undercurrent of panic in Cam's voice, because he made it out to the house in twenty minutes flat.

"I understand why you want to play this close to your vest," he said after Cam had given him a brief summary of recent events. "I'll use my car phone to initiate a routine check of all your domestic employees. That shouldn't arouse suspicion."

Cam agreed—anything to make himself feel as if he were taking some action.

Noel, who had to travel from Light Street, arrived as Jason was returning to the house. She gave Cam a fierce hug as soon as she learned about Jo's abduction. "I'm so sorry. But I'm glad you trusted us to help you," she whispered.

He nodded tightly and turned away, afraid that he was going to break down in front of his friends. In front of O'Malley, for that matter.

"Why don't you fill in some details?" Jason suggested.

Cam swallowed hard, grateful for the matter-of-fact tone. The only way he could get through this was to tell it straight—as if it had happened to someone else. As if some other woman had been kidnapped. Not his wife.

"You woke up on the lawn less than an hour ago?" Noel clarified as they sat grim faced around the kitchen table. "Are you okay?"

"The effects have pretty much worn off," he lied. He wasn't going to let a pounding headache slow him down.

Noel looked from Cam to Jason. "I don't think I quite have the whole picture. I knew Jo was upset about something big the day I was out here. What have the three of you been hiding from me?"

"Jo got a series of letters threatening me and Randolph Electronics," Cam answered, filling Jason in on her motivation. Then he went on to tell Noel about the wave compressor.

"A few years ago I would have had a pretty good idea who might try to pull off a job like this," Jason muttered.

"Yeah, the industrial espionage business changes fast," Cam said, but he didn't catch the worried look that Noel and Jason exchanged. "If those thugs were sent here to get my invention, why didn't they take me?"

"They may have been instructed to get both you and Jo. But they weren't prepared for every contingency. When you came out with a gun, you took them by surprise."

The phone rang and Jason instantly switched gears. "Have you set up recording equipment?"

"Damn. I—"

"Recording software operational," a voice cut in from the intercom speaker. It sounded as if it were hooked up to Cam's computer. He knew it had to be O'Malley. At least the ghost was good for something.

He pushed a button that would receive the call over his speaker system.

"Cameron Randolph?" The voice was just as mechanical as the one from the intercom. It was undoubtedly being altered electronically so there was no chance of recognizing or tracing the person on the other end of the line.

Cam's heart was racing as he answered in a remarkably steady voice. "Speaking."

"I have your wife."

"Who are you?"

"You don't need to know that yet."

He might have been alone in the room. All his attention was focused on the telephone speaker. "Jo had better be all right."

"I'm afraid you're not in any position to make demands."

Cam detected a slight blurring of the words, maybe a thick accent that the computer scrambling couldn't quite hide.

"If she's not in perfect condition, you're not getting a damn thing out of me."

"Say hello to your husband," the voice commanded.

"Oh!" Jo gasped as if someone had tiptoed up behind her and clapped his hands loudly.

"Honey. Thank God. Are you all right?" At the sound of her voice, a silent prayer welled up inside him. His worst nightmare had been that she might be dead.

"I'm okay," she said with a tremor she was probably trying hard to control. "It must have been a tranquilizer gun. I just woke up a little while ago." She gulped audibly.

He could picture the strained expression on her face. "Where are you?"

"In... in... a bedroom."

"Is anyone with you?" he asked sharply.

"No." She paused for several seconds as if inspecting unfamiliar surroundings. "I'm... I'm alone. I guess there's some kind of speaker in here, but I can't find it," she said, the end of the sentence rising on a note of panic.

He needed to take her in his arms, lie to her and tell her that everything was going to be okay. Most important, he couldn't let her know how frightened he was. "It's okay, honey. We'll get you out of this."

"My head hurts. It's hard to think straight."

"I know." He rubbed his own temple, wishing it didn't throb.

"Oh, Cam, you were right about my getting out of town. I should have listened to you," she said plaintively.

"Everything's going to be fine," he reassured her, praying that it was true.

The mechanical voice interrupted. "For obvious reasons, we're not going to stay on the line much longer."

"Who are you?" Jo demanded.

The speaker ignored her. "Listen to me closely, Randolph. You will not contact the police. You will pack up your wave-compressing equipment and load it into an unmarked van. You will stand by for instructions about where to proceed next. And you will make sure you're not followed, because if you try to lead the authorities to my location or involve your associate Jason Zacharias in this matter, your wife will die a very slow, painful death. Do you understand?"

He heard Jo gasp, and his gaze shot to Jason. Lord, he'd already made a fatal mistake if the man on the other end of the line found out Jason was here. Anger and frustration made his hands ball into fists.

"Do you get the message?"

"Yes," he spat out, fighting to see through the murderous red haze that spread across his vision.

"Excellent. And don't bother to think about coming armed. You and your equipment will be very thoroughly searched when you arrive here. I will be contacting you within the next few hours."

The phone line went dead, leaving Cam feeling as if he'd been punched in the stomach. Moments later, the intercom crackled. "We have his phone number."

"Oh, God. Cam." Noel scrambled out of her seat and came to him, wrapping her arms around his shoulders and pulling him against her breast like a mother comforting a child who'd been hurt.

He couldn't stop himself from clinging to her, wishing she were Jo, struggling to hold himself together.

Over his shoulder, he looked at Jason. "How does he know about you?" he asked when he could make his voice work reasonably well.

"The bastard's been poking about in your personal life and private business for months, or he couldn't have pulled this off."

"Yeah. So you'd better leave before he finds out you're here."

"Cam, he obviously doesn't know I'm here. We can—"

His head snapped up and his eyes drilled into Jason. "Are you deaf? He doesn't want you involved. I let him take her. Now *I* have to figure out how to get her back."

"You did everything humanly possible to stop him."

Cam ignored the reassurance. "I can't do anything besides what he says. I can't take a chance on his hurting Jo. It sounds like he's going to swap the wave-generating equipment for her."

"You can't count on that. Is it operational?"

"No. I haven't exactly had the time to work on it recently."

"I'd assume he's going to keep you until it's working. Then both of you are expendable—because you'll know too much about him."

"I *have* to cooperate," he repeated, his voice bleak with anguish.

"As long as he thinks you're going along with his plans, he won't hurt her. At least let me find out how the gardening service was infiltrated—" Jason began.

"Don't you get it? The two of you have to leave and pretend you haven't heard from me."

"Cam, you're not thinking rationally," Jason argued.

"Get out!"

Chapter Twelve

Silence hung in the room like thick, choking smoke. Cam looked at the faces of the two people who had dropped what they were doing and rushed to his house—even when they hadn't known what had happened. "I'm sorry. I know you're trying to help both of us."

Noel smoothed her hand across his shoulder. "I understand. You're upset. You're afraid for Jo."

"Yeah." He struggled to make his drugged brain function logically. The kidnapper *would* have worded his threat differently if he'd known anyone else was here. Given that assumption, it was foolish to toss out the tremendous asset of having Jason Zacharias on his team. Jason was one of the top security experts in the country. He'd worked on kidnappings before, most recently helping their friends Steve and Abby rescue their baby daughter from international terrorists. Cam sucked in a deep breath and let it out slowly. He'd trust Jason with his life, but what about Jo's life? When he looked up, he found Jason and Noel watching him anxiously. "I still think I have to go in there alone. But maybe you can provide me with some backup."

His friend nodded. "I won't do a thing without your authorization. But let's talk about some options. Say the word and we can have a SWAT team on standby. You can bring in a couple of microsatellite emitters."

"How?"

"In your watch and your energy compressor. Then push the button whenever you're ready for us."

"How long will it take you to get set up?"

"A couple of hours for the SWAT team. But modifications to the DOD satellite tracking system are going to take eight to ten hours minimum."

"You're absolutely sure you can do all that without word getting back to the kidnappers?" Cam's gaze probed Jason's as he spoke.

"I know what's on the line, and I won't let you down," Jason promised. "Everything will be kept at a top-secret level. We'll—"

Cam held up a warning hand. "Don't tell me any more about your speculations or your plans. If I'm asked, I have to be able to answer truthfully that I'm acting entirely on my own. I'm just praying the kidnapper doesn't find out you've been here."

"He thinks you didn't have time to bring in reinforcements because he was monitoring Jo and called you right after she woke up." Jason made the speculation sound like gospel. "Either you got a lower dose of the tranquilizer, or your constitution's stronger."

Or a ghost was bellowing at me, Cam thought. But he only nodded.

"How did you pick up the phone number so quickly?" Jason asked. "Do you have some experimental phone-tracing equipment that I don't know about?"

"I think we'd better not discuss the details."

"He's right," Noel said. "He has to convince the man who called that he's following instructions."

"Then let's get going," Jason said. "If you give me the phone number, I'll try to get a location."

Cam scribbled the digits on a notepad. "This looks like one of those national cellular numbers. Probably unlisted and owned by some dummy corporation. But give it a shot, anyway. Meanwhile, if anyone asks, tell them that Jo and I were called out of town suddenly on a business trip."

Jason nodded tightly. "What if that guy Crowley calls from the Defense Department?"

"Stall him just like everybody else," Cam said tersely.

Before they left, Noel gave him another tight hug. Then he was alone in the mansion.

No, not alone, he thought with a grimace.

FOR A LONG TIME Jo sat with her head bent and her arms wrapped around her slender shoulders, wishing that Cam were the one holding her. It was impossible to stop her body from trembling.

In a barely audible voice, she whispered Cam's name.

Of course, no one answered.

The phone call had been a lifeline. When the connection had snapped, she'd felt as if a piece of herself had been cut away, leaving her more alone and frightened than she'd ever been in her life—even when Art Nugent had taken her hostage three years ago. Then she'd given herself the illusion she was doing something to help Cam find her. This time was different.

In some part of her mind, she knew why it was so hard to cope, why she felt so utterly vulnerable and helpless. The dregs of a tranquilizer were still sloshing around in her brain cells. So she was fighting her reaction to the drug as much as she was fighting her own fear. What made it ten times worse was the knowledge that if she'd trusted Cam's judgment, she wouldn't be in this mess.

A wave of remorse and dizziness swept over her. It was all she could do to stop herself from rolling to her side, pulling her knees up to her chin and closing her eyes. Maybe this was all a drug-induced bad dream. A punishment for flinging that crack about their marriage at Cam. The simple solution was to go back to sleep. When she woke up again, this nightmare would be over, and she'd be back in her own bed with Cam. Every fiber of her being longed to cling to that reassuring fantasy.

But she knew she wasn't dreaming. Grimly she dug her fingernails into her palms, welcoming the pain because it helped her clear her head. She had to face the facts. She'd been taken from home hours ago. She was in an underground room. And the man who had kidnapped her was probably watching her now and taking notes on her mental state.

That chilling thought was the thing that got her moving. She sucked in a steadying breath and let it out slowly. Then she pushed herself off the bed and walked to the door. It was still locked. So she methodically began to search the rest of the room, trying to find something she'd overlooked, or some scrap of information that would help her improve her odds. The second inspection only reinforced her first impression. She was in a high-security cell that had been given a cosmetic veneer.

She was going through the toiletries in the medicine cabinet when she heard the lock click. She froze.

The door slowly opened, and a figure clad in black stepped into the room.

"I see you're feeling better."

Because of the position of the mirror, she couldn't make out his features clearly. What she saw must be some nasty trick of the lighting.

She stood with her hands gripping the edge of the sink.

"I think it's time we met face-to-face," he rasped. "Turn around."

She didn't want to obey, but she knew she had to find out the worst. When she looked him full in the face, a scream rose in her throat.

WITH LEADEN STEPS, Cam headed for his lab and began to check the wave-compressor equipment, wondering how long he had to pack and where he'd be going.

"Don't disconnect it yet." The voice he'd been dreading broke the silence as O'Malley materialized in the center of the room.

Cam turned back toward the machinery. "I have to be ready to leave when he calls."

"You can explain you ran into a hitch."

"No."

"He'll take your word for it."

"Listen, O'Malley, you're the one who said you came back to help Jo. Stop putting her life in danger."

"I'm offering you an advantage he won't be expecting."

He gave the apparition a direct look. "Like what?"

There was a pleading expression on the ghost's face. "Take me with you. I have powers he won't be able to fight."

"You said you couldn't leave the house."

"I was thinking about it while you were on the phone. There might be a way."

"Can you transfer your energy pattern into my equipment?" Cam asked, a spark of hope leaping in his breast.

"No."

"Then what are we talking about?"

The ghost hesitated for several seconds. "Something more personal. Take me along as a passenger. In your body. If my consciousness is folded into yours, I could go where you go."

"That's . . . crazy."

"No, it isn't."

"Have you ever done something like that before?"

"No."

"So you have no idea whether it will work," Cam enunciated carefully, as if he were talking to a first-year graduate student who had proposed to build an apartment complex in noneuclidean space. "Or whether you can operate your powers from a physical staging platform. Or whether you'll kill me in the attempt to come into my body, for that matter."

There was another long silence. "All of that is true. But it's almost certain you're going on a suicide mission, anyway. If you just hand over your invention to the kidnapper, the chances are he's going to kill you and Jo the minute you have the system operational."

Cam rubbed his throbbing temples. "I may be able to rig something when I get a look at his layout. Or I may be able to get Jo out of there somehow—even if I don't make it."

"I could give you the chance you need to save both of you," Skip argued.

To give himself time to think, Cam powered up the wave generator and slowly adjusted the setting to the ones he'd been using when he'd first brought his uninvited houseguest into focus.

He could feel the apparition waiting tensely for his answer. Let him stew for a few minutes. He was asking a hell of a lot—given the risks. Cam thought about their uneasy relationship up to now. Both of them loved Jo. Both of them wanted her. If he let O'Malley have the kind of access to his mind and body he was asking for, it was like handing him the perfect opportunity to get rid of his rival. He shuddered, then pictured the smug expression on O'Malley's face after he pulled off that coup. Was he capable of such ruthlessness? Such duplicity? He'd certainly enjoyed bamboozling Frankie's sister. Had he ever murdered anyone?

Cam didn't know the man. He certainly didn't trust him. But he could imagine the degree of his desperation. And he knew he had nothing to lose and everything to gain.

In one quick stroke O'Malley could put himself into position to win Jo back. Have a second chance. Cam tried to imagine how Jo would react when she realized what had happened. The angry words she'd flung at him before stomping out of the house rang in his ears. In his present torment, he had to clench his teeth to keep from screaming out his despair.

Jo was a woman of strong feelings. She'd loved Skip O'Malley with her heart and soul, because she was capable of no less. She'd mourned his loss. After all these years, she'd never even given up his name. And Cam had seen the way she'd been pulled back into the emotions of the past when her dead husband had materialized.

Had she come around to thinking she'd rather try again with O'Malley? Go back to her old life-style where the two of them could take all the dangerous assignments they wanted? The speculation was like acid burning inside him. He tried to force his mind into a safer channel, but he'd been through so many shocks in the past few days that he wasn't capable of emotional control.

He hoped the ghost couldn't see the grim expression on his face. He'd be a fool to let a ham-handed jerk like O'Malley anywhere near his body—or his wife. Yet . . .

He dragged in a steadying breath. He loved Jo. He'd vowed to fight tooth and nail to keep her. But what if he had to give up his life to save hers? What if the ghost were right? Whatever else O'Malley had in mind, his proposal might be the only way to rescue the woman they both loved.

"You want me to let you share my body?" he asked. "That's taking a pretty big chance since you hate my guts."

"I don't hate you."

"Just a minute. Let's get our facts straight. You tried to kill me the night Jo came down to the lab to make love."

O'Malley grimaced. "I wasn't handling my jealousy very well. I saw you with her, and I freaked out."

"Yeah. Right. So this could be a golden opportunity for you. You could get rid of me and step right into my life with Jo."

"You'd have to trust me not to do that."

"I'd be a fool to trust you."

"It's a damn sight better than walking defenseless into the kidnapper's trap."

"For the sake of argument, let's assume you're on the level. Suppose we try your insane suggestion, and you accidentally knock me off. Then we leave Jo at that bastard's mercy."

"Maybe we can both arrange to haunt him."

Cam laughed hollowly. But he was reassured by the false bravado in the ghost's voice. If O'Malley was worried, maybe he wasn't planning anything sinister.

"We're wasting time. Do you want to give it a shot or not?"

"I need some facts so I can make an informed decision. What can you tell me about the process?"

"Nothing. I'll just have to try a couple of things."

Cam clenched his fists, fighting anger and frustration. If he went ahead with this plan it would be on blind faith.

In the end, he knew he had no other choices. Wearily he nodded at the apparition.

"All right. You win. What do you want me to do?"

The ghostly image suddenly looked a lot less confident. "Well, turn up the equipment, so I'll be able to draw on the energy if I need it."

Cam walked to the apparatus and adjusted several dials.

"This could be, uh, stressful. Probably you'd better lie down."

"That will make it convenient when they find the body." Stalking back into the office, Cam stretched out on the couch and closed his eyes. He sensed O'Malley hovering over him almost as if he were a physical presence.

"Get it over with!"

For several seconds nothing happened. Then he felt invisible fingers probing into his mind. At first the touch was tentative. Then the grip became more firm. He hadn't known it would be like this! His whole body rebelled, and he tried to fight against the alien presence with every fiber of his will. But he was powerless to stop the probing. It went deeper, wider, shredding the neural connections in his brain tissue like so much tissue paper.

A low, animal scream of terror gurgled in his throat as he struggled to hold together the fabric of what was Cameron Randolph. But his will was not enough. He felt himself shattering into a million pieces like the detonation of a nuclear warhead. His personality was floating like dust in the mushroom cloud. Then miraculously, just as the fallout was about to scatter to the four winds, the invasion lessened.

He lay on the couch, unable to do more than suck air into his lungs. "Stop! You're killing me," he gasped out.

"Because you're resisting me." The alien presence still clawed at the edge of his mind.

"Of course I'm resisting you! You're tearing my psyche apart. Do you have any idea what that feels like?"

"I told you, I haven't done this before. I may not be handling it right."

"You're not!"

"Let me see if I can go slower."

The only way Cam could lie still for another assault was by focusing on Jo. She was alone. Frightened. And he was the only one who could rescue her. "Go ahead," he whispered, bracing himself for the ordeal. This time he felt a tiny tendril of alien consciousness probing him, worming its way into his brain tissue.

It was a much more measured invasion. Still, every nerve ending in his body began to prickle as if ants were crawling over his skin.

"I won't hurt you," O'Malley whispered in his mind.

"You already are." He gasped, and his arms and legs jerked uncontrollably as waves of unendurable pain swept over him.

He was doing this for Jo. But no man should be asked to die in such agony. If he could have made his muscles work, he would have jumped up and fled the room. Fled the house where the demon torturing him couldn't follow. But an invisible force pinned him to the sofa, preventing his escape.

Something snapped, and he felt a burst of mortar shells exploding in his head.

"No. God, no," he screamed. Unaware of what he was doing or who he was, he began to pull on his hair, as if that would make the pain go away. Or maybe he was trying to pull O'Malley out of his mind.

He was empty. So empty. Then another presence was pouring into him like scalding coffee filling up a thermos bottle.

It sloshed and bubbled in his mind, burning through delicate tissue. Drowning conscious thoughts.

He lay panting for breath, feeling his heart pounding at a pace no one could sustain. He was dying. The tiny part of him that could still think knew that.

"No!" He howled his rage and terror. O'Malley had tricked him, after all. Or maybe they were both going down in flames. And no one would be left to save Jo.

Jo. He tried to hang on to the image of the woman he loved. It was all he had left. He saw her laughing in the sunlight as she showed him a bed of flowers she'd just planted. Saw her bent over her computer, so absorbed in her work that she didn't know he was there. Saw her standing in the garden surrounded by flowers, holding out her hand to him.

He reached toward her. But even as he did, she slipped away into a bank of gray mist.

Then there was only a terrible darkness so vast that he knew he would never climb out of it.

HE WAS DREAMING, but he didn't want it to be a dream. He was staring at Jo. She stood naked and beautiful and oh so seductive in the Jacuzzi down by the summer-house, holding out her hand to him, swaying toward him. Her lips moved. He strained to hear words that couldn't reach him through the transparent barrier that separated them.

But he didn't need to hear. He could read her lips.

"I love you. I need you."

Thank God! He'd been so afraid he'd lost her. He took an eager step toward her, but the transparent curtain stopped his progress as the dream shifted into a nightmare. He raised his hands, pounding with his fists. They punched into something soft. Yet it was thick and strong. It held him back as easily as iron bars.

"Jo, I'm sorry I messed things up."

She looked sad. "It wasn't you. It was my fault." By painful degrees, the sadness in her eyes gave way to panic.

"Please. I'm afraid. Don't leave me here with the monster," she begged.

"What monster?" he shouted.

She didn't hear him. Instead she glanced quickly over her shoulder, and he saw a door materialize in what had looked like a hedge of fir trees. It opened just a crack, and she shrank away, trying to make herself small and inconspicuous. But the door opened wider, and a slug-like hand reached through. Reached for her.

She scrambled out of the water and rushed forward, heading for him. Just before she reached him, relief suffused her features. In the next second, the transparent curtain stopped her, and she began to tear at it frantically with her fingers.

He could see her screaming in terror. But he couldn't hear.

"Jo, oh, Jo." He pressed his palms against the barrier. She saw his hands and flattened hers out, too. They stood palm to palm, close but separated by a tissue-thin film. Tears leaked from her eyes and trickled down her cheeks.

Darkness came from the opening behind her. Like a black hole in space, it swallowed up everything. First Jo. Then himself.

He couldn't see. But he could still feel the pressure of her palm. Then even that slender contact with her was gone, and his consciousness winked out.

HIS EYES FLUTTERED OPEN. He blinked, trying to bring the room into focus through the strange double vision that made his head spin. He was lying on the sofa in his office. The room was entirely familiar to him, yet it was also entirely strange.

He sucked in a draft of air and let it out slowly, feeling the movement of his lungs as if breathing in and out weren't something that happened ten times a minute.

Caught up in the wonder of simple physical sensations, he stroked his hand across the corduroy fabric of the cushions. Such an ordinary thing, but he couldn't get over the way the fibers moved under his fingers and tickled his nerve endings.

God, I'd forgotten what the world feels like. What it feels like to breathe. What a heartbeat feels like.

The words came from within his head. But he hadn't voiced the thought.

Every cell in his body went rigid.

It's me.

"O'Malley," he breathed.

You remember what happened?

He remembered searing pain. And the dream about Jo. And blackness. "You're...with me."

Yes.

He sat up and looked around the room, trying to sort things out. He knew who he was. Thank God, he was still Cameron Randolph. Thirty-eight years old. Inventor. President of Randolph Electronics. Husband of Jo O'Malley.

The last thought brought a stab of pain. Regret. Confusion.

Husband to Jo O'Malley. They were both her husband. Cameron Randolph and Skip O'Malley. In the dream, they had both lunged toward her. Both felt the panic of not being able to break through the invisible barrier. All at once he knew that was how O'Malley had felt ever since he'd come back to earth. Separated from any physical sensations by a transparent membrane.

Cam dragged in a shuddering breath. By the same token, there was no way to hide *his* feelings from the presence hovering in his brain. O'Malley knew everything about him. Every hope. Every fear. Every private, shameful, self-serving impulse that he'd censored from the scrutiny of the world. All of it was out in the open like a raw, aching nerve.

When he tried to cut off the flow of thoughts, an incident he'd long forgotten leapt into his mind. It was in

fifth grade when he and Rob Dorsey had hated each
other's guts. He'd taken a penknife and carved Rob's
initials into his desk, because he knew that would get
him in trouble with Miss McClure. Only Rob knew exactly who had done it. So he did the same thing to Cam.
And they'd both spent the next ten detention hours
sanding and refinishing their desks.

He didn't know why that ancient memory had zinged
back to him now. And he didn't like O'Malley's snort
of derision. In retaliation, he plunged into the other
man's consciousness and found an even more savory
morsel. When O'Malley had been sixteen, his girl-
friend's parents had come home early from a party and
discovered the two kids half-naked, making out on the
couch.

Cam laughed at the wave of embarrassment that
swept toward him, or was it through him. O'Malley
glowered. And the duel was on. It was a unique way for
two men who hated each other to battle. Like street
fighters slashing at each other with knives, they gashed
and hacked, ducked and tried to hide in the shadows.
But there was no place to flee from each other. They
were bound together—Siamese twins joined at the
brain.

With a vengeance, they got around to the real issue
between them. Cam ferreted out what he'd suspected.
That Jo had been the best thing in Skip O'Malley's life,
felt his amazement that a woman so young could want
a beaten up old P.I. Not to be outdone, O'Malley
glommed on to every personal detail of Jo's marriage
to Cam, including the recent passionate scene in her
Mustang.

To block it out, Cam went on the attack, digging into O'Malley's deepest insecurities. "And you just stood there and watched them cart Jo away."

The ghost came back with a similar taunt. *Deep down you know you can't rescue Jo by yourself. You were just trying to sound confident for Zacharias.*

The war went on until they were both worn-out—and disgusted by what they'd just done. By mutual agreement, they tried to stay on the surface of each other's mind. But it didn't help much. Cam and O'Malley knew each other more intimately than any two human beings in the history of the world. And they both hated it.

Cam cursed under his breath, unsure he could cope with the naked embarrassment of his exposure to his rival. But he didn't have much choice.

I'm sorry, I didn't know it was going to be this bad, the other man whispered in his brain.

"Sure." He didn't have to speak aloud. All he had to do was start to think a thought, and O'Malley had access to it. Somehow vocalizing fostered the illusion of separation.

Look on the positive side. We both made it.

"I thought you wanted to snatch my body."

I know. He paused, and Cam cringed at the question forming in his mind. *So are you going to let me see if I can take control?*

Control of this joint entity. He didn't bother to try to hide the new terror that leapt in his chest. But he didn't protest. He had come too far not to take the logical next step.

He didn't ask what he had to do. He knew. Leaning back into the cushions, he closed his eyes and tried to empty his mind of thought the way he did before he went to sleep.

It wasn't easy. Not with fear gnawing at his insides. But there came a point where Cameron Randolph began to leak away like a balloon losing air from a dozen holes.

He tried to staunch the flow. The task was impossible. One moment he was in control of his being. In the next, he was shoved back into some tiny corner of his mind as if he were only a visitor—no, a prisoner—in his own consciousness.

His body jerked as he tried to claw his way back to the surface.

Help. Don't do this to me.

"Oh, man. Oh, man." Skip O'Malley gave a joyous shout, stood and began to dance around the room like a lunatic just released from solitary confinement.

O'Malley dragged him around the office, laughing wildly, touching everything. His hand knocked against a coffee mug, sending it crashing to the floor. O'Malley didn't seem to notice.

Stop, Cam shouted inside his brain. *Take it easy.*

O'Malley paid no heed to his tiny voice. The simplest object was fodder for his delirium. He held up the paperweight that had been a Christmas present from Jo and stroked his fingers over the smooth surface. He dug out a cinnamon candy from the jar on the shelf and popped it into his mouth, smacking his lips in appreciation as the spicy flavor filled his mouth.

He threw the door open and marched into the lab, heading for the wave-compressor equipment.

Stop. What are you doing? Cam shouted.

The ghost in command of his body paid no attention. He pressed his hand against the CRT, closed his eyes and swayed to some pulsing rhythm only he could feel.

No, Cam admitted, he could feel it, too. It was like raw energy flowing into the cells of his body, charging them as though they were a storage battery.

He felt his face tingle, felt his skin stretch as if internal pressure might make him burst. He stared at his hands, expecting them to look like inflated rubber gloves. They seemed entirely normal. In fact, there were no outward signs that anything unusual was happening.

O'Malley let go of the equipment. For several seconds, nothing happened. Then sparks began to jump between Cam's hands.

Power crackled and sputtered from the machine to Cam and back again. O'Malley tried to discharge the energy, tried to hurl it away from his body. But he couldn't do it.

Cam felt his hair stand on end, felt the tingling of a dangerous current coursing through human flesh. *Help me.* Something snapped, and Cam was in control again. For all the good it did him.

Screaming in pain, he whirled, looking for anything that was grounded. The radio antenna. Clamping his fists on to the metal, he felt the electricity discharge through the wiring.

Then he slumped, panting, against the wall.

Sweat poured off his aching body.

His body. He was the dominant personality once again.

"Good going," he growled. "You almost killed me."

O'Malley didn't answer.

"Are you all right?"

No one replied.

He was alone, sitting with his back to the wall.

Chapter Thirteen

"O'Malley?"

There was no answer. Not from his mind. Not from anywhere else in the room. Staggering across the laboratory, Cam fiddled with the controls on the wave compressor, watching the readouts as he worked.

Nothing changed. The ghost that had haunted the lab was gone, and Cam felt a deep surge of relief as well as bitter disappointment. Having O'Malley in his mind, reading his most intimate thoughts, taking control of his actions when it suited him, was a soul-stripping experience. But he would have endured it for Jo's sake.

However, the ghost had miscalculated and done himself in. So much for his generous offer of help. Probably he was back where he belonged—at the entrance to the heavenly tunnel. And Cam was worse off than he had been an hour ago, because he'd lost precious time.

Automatically he began to pack up the equipment he was supposed to deliver to the kidnapper. But as he worked, some of O'Malley's arguments began to overlay his initial logic. After he delivered his equipment, he'd be trapped as effectively as Jo. And probably he wasn't going to be able to save either himself or her.

Was there some other way? Maybe he should call Jason back on the secure line and see what he'd found out.

He was heading toward the phone when it rang. Startled, he leapt for the receiver.

"Randolph." It was the same computerized speaker who had contacted him earlier.

"Yes."

"Are you ready to leave?"

"No."

"Why not?"

"The effects of your tranquilizer gun are slowing me down." It wasn't really a lie, it just wasn't the whole truth.

"You will leave within the hour or your wife will be very unhappy."

Cam's whole body went rigid—and not just from the overt threat. Even with the computer distortion, he heard a raggedness around the edges of the voice. The man sounded as if he were coming unglued. "If *anything* happens to Jo," he said very carefully, "you can forget about my cooperation."

"You're not in a position to make demands."

He ignored the threat. "Let me talk to Jo."

There was a heart-stopping pause. "I think you're stalling. But really, you're needed here urgently."

Cam's heart began to thud in his chest.

"Turn on your videophone," the voice commanded.

"How do you know I have one?"

The man cut him off with a sharp laugh that sent a tremor along Cam's spine. "I know a great deal about you, Dr. Randolph."

Teeth clenched, Cam turned toward the expensive piece of communications equipment he'd bought so he could talk face-to-face with the Randolph staff from home. When nothing appeared on the screen, he wondered if the kidnapper was simply playing a cruel joke. Then the monitor blinked. At first he couldn't believe the picture that seemed to shimmer before him like a scene in a horror movie.

The camera gave him several views of an underground dungeon with a stone floor and rough stone walls that oozed with moisture. Large metal sconces filled with white candles were spaced around at intervals, casting menacing shadows, making the whole place into a den of unspeakable fear. Then the angle changed. In the flickering light, he saw a woman and gasped.

"Jo," he cried out. But he didn't want it to be her. She was wearing a long white sleeveless dress, and she was chained to large rings spaced wide apart in the stone wall.

At the sound of his voice, she jerked and tried to pull her hands free from their bonds. Details came to him in flashes. He saw then that her wrists were circled by leather cuffs that fastened her firmly to the rings in the wall. "Cam? Is that you?"

"Oh, God, honey."

She raised her head.

"The camera's over to the right, lass. Up there on the wall."

When she stared pleadingly at him, he felt as if he were being torn apart from the inside out. "You bastard. Let her go."

"As the saying goes, a picture is worth a thousand words. I want you to understand just how much your wife needs you here with her."

"Let her go!"

"You're the only one who can do that."

Cam swore vehemently, still not fully able to believe what he was watching.

He sensed that Jo wasn't alone in the room. She tried to cringe away from a shadowy figure outside the camera's range, but the bonds prevented her escape.

"No!" Cam shouted, his voice rising in desperation as he leapt toward the image of Jo, clawing at the screen as if he could pull her through it and into the safety of his arms. But she was beyond his reach.

At the same time, Jo's control snapped. "Please. Don't."

Seething, barely able to contain himself, he balled his hands into fists.

The man off camera spoke to her. "Tell him to hurry," he murmured. "Before something unfortunate happens to you."

Jo stared at the camera. Her lips were trembling, but her eyes were amazingly steady. "Cam, don't come here."

"Not a very wise suggestion, Mrs. Randolph."

The last thing he saw before the connection snapped was Jo's eyes filled with terror.

Cam was left gasping for breath, praying that what he'd just seen was some kind of hallucination. Madness was preferable to reality. But he knew his mind wasn't playing sadistic tricks. He'd been given a glimpse into hell.

JO'S SKIN CRAWLED as her captor stared at her.

"Do you know what a chance you're taking by defying me?" he asked in a deceptively soft voice.

Jo swallowed hard.

"Answer me!"

"No."

"You're either a fool or a liar."

He glided closer to her.

With every fiber of her being, she struggled not to shudder. Not to break down. Because her defiance was all she had left, and if she let go and started to scream she might not be able to stop.

"You'd better hope your husband gets here soon." Her captor stood staring at her for long, agonizing moments. Then he turned on his heels and left the dungeon cell, shutting the heavy door firmly behind him.

Jo sagged against the stone wall in relief. It was cold and clammy, but she needed the support to stay on her feet.

Closing her eyes, she struggled for the calm center of her soul. She had been in tight spots before.

This time was different. This man had done his homework. He was smart. He was determined to obtain what he wanted. He was full of hatred. And he was insane.

She shuddered violently and tried to wrench herself away from the wall. All she did was hurt her wrists—and remind herself that he could come walking back in the door at any moment and do anything he wanted to her.

CAM STOOD PARALYZED, his heart pounding, his mind churning. Then he jerked back to life. He had to get to Jo. He had to finish packing the equipment and load it into his van. At first he moved like an automaton, hardly aware of what he was doing. Slowly the physical work helped calm him. By the time he was finished packing, he was thinking clearly again. He wanted to leave at once, but he forced himself to take a few more precious minutes.

Stepping into the office, he booted up the computer and inserted a video disk. After setting it to record, he faced the camera built into the wall unit and gave a concise summary of what had happened over the past few days—amazed that he could filter out his ire and his fear as he talked. Included was a detailed scientific proof of his work on the wave compressor and a formal request to initiate legal proceedings against anyone else who brought the process to market using his techniques. He put one copy of the recording into the wall safe, which would be opened by his executor in the event of his death.

The other he put into an envelope addressed to Jason with instructions to open it if his friend hadn't heard from him within five days.

Finally, with a few keystrokes, he executed a command that destroyed all the files in his home computer. Anything critical was duplicated at Randolph Electronics, where it ought to be secure. The important thing was that if the kidnapper killed him, he wouldn't be able to raid his notes.

He was on the road when he phoned the designated number. The call was answered immediately. "Where have you been?" a new voice snapped.

"I'm heading for the beltway."

"Proceed up I-70 to Frederick. Take 340 toward Charlestown. You will be contacted with further instructions."

On the road to Charlestown, he was directed toward Harper's Ferry, West Virginia, where he was told to pull into one of the parking lots along the Potomac River.

As he drove, the scene from the dungeon kept leaping into his thoughts. He saw again the terror on Jo's face. And heard her plea for him not to come there. Oh

God, if he'd ever doubted she loved him, that heartfelt request erased all uncertainty. She was alone and frightened. But she wanted to keep him safe.

His hands clenched on the wheel. If that bastard hurt her, he'd personally tear him apart.

Five minutes after he found the parking area, a gray van took the space next to his. A man in putty-colored coveralls got out and approached him without hesitation. "Dr. Randolph, I'm your driver. I'll help you load the equipment."

He didn't waste his breath asking questions or directing his anger toward a flunky; he simply transferred boxes from one van to the other.

"You're to ride in the back," the driver said. "And I have instructions to take your watch."

Cam gave the driver a sharp look before he slipped off his Rolex. Did he know something, or was it just a precaution so Cam wouldn't be able to judge the duration of the trip? In any case, without the watch, he was down to one emitter.

Alone in the back of the windowless van, he was enveloped by panic. Somehow he brought the terrible fear under control. The monster had only wanted to frighten him into compliance, he told himself. He wouldn't hurt Jo. He wouldn't. The only way he could keep his sanity was to tell himself that over and over.

Finally the van came to a stop, and he felt his heart rate jump as he heard machinery grinding. When the van opened, he found himself in what looked like the underground parking facility at a hotel or office building, only not as large.

The driver ushered him toward a door marked Warning—Automatic Alarm System.

The moment after he stepped into a long corridor, he heard metal clank shut behind him like a prison gate. A series of TV cameras followed his progress as he strode rapidly up the hallway, hoping his face didn't betray the sick feeling in the pit of his stomach. He wanted to appear in control, but his steps quickened so that he was finally running and gasping for breath.

Another door loomed ahead of him. Beyond was a flight of stone steps leading down into darkness. Down into the dungeon where he had seen Jo. He took the steps two at a time. When he reached the bottom, he called her name.

"Cam, is that you?"

Her muffled voice came from farther ahead and to his left.

"Yes. It's me. I'm coming, honey."

Every nerve in his body screamed in silent anguish as he ran.

"Cam. Oh, please. Cam."

Her voice rose in panic. The naked fear made him want to bellow out his rage. Near the end of the hall, he found her in the cell he'd seen.

"Merciful God." She was still chained to the wall. His fingers were thick as he fumbled with the heavy lever that held the door fast. The lock rasped, and he rushed into the dark interior toward her small, vulnerable figure.

Her face was set in a defiant mask, but he could see how much effort the show of bravery had cost her.

Cursing in rage, he reached for the catch on her right wrist. His hands were shaking so badly that it seemed to take forever to release her.

Freed at last, she collapsed against him, clutching at his shoulders, trying to make her body part of his. He gathered her to him, cradling her like something rare and precious.

They were both trembling, both drawing in great gasps of air as they clung to each other.

"Jo. Oh, honey, I'm so sorry," he told her over and over, needing to hold her as much as she needed the safety of his arms.

"Not your fault. You shouldn't have come. I got you into this trap—"

"No."

"Cam. I love you. I love you."

"I love *you*."

She finally broke, the sobs racking her slender body. She felt so fragile in his arms, but there was nothing he could do but clasp her to him.

"I should have come faster." He kissed her hair, her forehead, her cheeks and finally her mouth. Then he drew back and gave her a careful inspection. She was pale as death, but he saw no evidence that she'd been hurt.

She pressed her face into his shoulder, as if she could shut out the horror of this place. He wanted, with every fiber of his being, to take her away. He knew there was no easy escape. Everything had been planned too well. Every evasion anticipated.

"Who did this to you?"

"He—"

"I believe it would be more appropriate for you to address yourself to me," a sharp voice cut her off.

Cam felt the hairs on the back of his neck stand on end. Thrusting Jo behind him as if his body could protect her, he turned.

A man stood in the doorway, his face concealed by a hood, his figure bent and twisted. It would be easy to take him, Cam thought, his whole body tensing to spring. Then he saw the dark figure was backed up by two muscular guards, each of them armed with pistols.

"What are you hiding?" Cam growled.

The man reached for the hem of the black fabric and pulled it slowly up as if he were unveiling a piece of prize sculpture.

Jo cringed in anticipation. Unable to take his gaze away, Cam watched, transfixed by the face that was revealed inch by inch. Maybe it had once been handsome. Certainly it had once been human. Now the features were blurred and melted together as if the skin were plastic and had been distorted by the cruel flame of a blowtorch.

Cam struggled to maintain his composure.

The hideous face contorted into what might have been meant as a smile. "Your mother must have taught you excellent manners, Dr. Randolph. Most people can't repress a little gasp of horror when they first make my acquaintance."

"You have me at a disadvantage."

"I know that, laddie."

"Do you have a name?"

"Sir Douglas Frye."

Cam stared at the ruined face and the twisted figure before him, hardly able to believe what he'd just heard. Jason had told him about the powerful information broker, Sir Douglas Frye, who had blackmailed world governments and corporate leaders alike with the dirt he'd collected. Working undercover, Jason had brought the man's empire down around his ears—and Frye had blown up his castle from his underground control room rather than allow himself to be captured. Jason and everybody else had thought he was dead. Could he really have survived? Lord, if this was the same man, then they were dealing with absolute evil. And madness, judging from the raging look in his eyes.

"Frye... but you were killed two years ago in Scotland," Jo said.

"It's a definite advantage to have your enemies believe that they've sent you on to greener pastures. Then when you pop back into circulation, they don't know who you're up against."

"But—but how did you get away?" Jo asked.

"I don't divulge my escape routes." His voice turned hard. "I believe the chitchat is concluded until we all meet at dinner. Dr. Randolph, your equipment has been transferred to the laboratory you'll be using. So it's time for you to get to it."

"My wife is coming with me."

"I think not."

"I think you want me to concentrate on my work, and I won't be able to do that if I'm worried about Jo."

The two men stared at each other. Finally Frye shrugged. "We'll see how well you tend to business with her sitting quietly in a corner. If you don't make significant progress, we'll try other arrangements tomorrow."

Cam slowly let out the breath he was holding, grateful for the small victory, yet wondering if he was going to have another.

"By the way, lad, if you've brought along other signaling devices like the one in your watch, you'll find them totally useless." The older man's lips curved up into a smug smile. "Our underground facility provides level-one shielding."

The breath froze in Cam's lungs, and he shot Frye a startled glance. But the man spared him barely a second look. After all those warnings, now that he had them both, he was so confident of his power that he wasn't even angry about the attempted security breach. Either Frye was a megalomaniac, or he knew he had them well and truly trapped, no matter what they tried.

AS THE PARTY MADE its way down the hall, Jo looked up and, for the first time, saw the face of one of the guards. He had reptilian skin and close-set eyes. And he was staring at her with a satisfied look.

"What?" Cam asked as he felt her body go rigid.

"He's the man I was following down at the warehouse," she managed to say.

"Aye," Frye cut in. "Donnel was on special assignment for me."

"*You* lured me down there," Jo accused.

"Precisely."

"But why would you send a series of notes warning about...about...yourself?"

He laughed harshly. "I didn't. The correspondence was initiated by Mr. Crowley from the Defense Department."

"What?" Cam's surprised exclamation rang out.

"Aye. He was glad to take my money to set you up. Then he had an attack of conscience. But he knew you'd turn him in the minute you suspected anything, so he tried to warn your wife. I just took advantage of the contact he established. He sent the first note. The second and third were from me—to set the ambush up so I could get your car."

"Crowley's right about my reaction," Cam muttered.

"If it's any consolation, he's a dead man."

Jo shuddered.

"Too bad you had the computer equipment in the car booby-trapped. You might not be here now," Frye added.

He turned and led the way down the hall, limping slightly. Jo glanced at Cam questioningly, and he shook his head. So he didn't believe Frye's claim. The man was just needling them.

"Come on." Donnel gave Jo a shove, and she clutched Cam's arm to keep from falling. She kept a tight hold on him, aware that her fingers were digging into his flesh. But she couldn't loosen her grip.

"I didn't want you to come, but I'm glad you're here," she whispered.

"You will not talk to each other!" Frye snapped without bothering to turn around.

Cam slipped his arm around Jo's shoulders and she cleaved to him, silently trying to tell him what a fool she'd been and how much she loved him. They climbed several flights of stone steps and came out in a part of the building she hadn't seen before.

She longed to tell Cam the few things she'd figured out, but she kept her lips pressed together.

"In here."

Frye pushed open a door halfway down another corridor. Jo followed Cam into a large room. Like every other part of the complex she'd seen, it was windowless. But bright fluorescent lights illuminated an amazingly well-stocked laboratory similar to the one Cam had set up at home. All his equipment was arranged on tables, and there were banks of other machines that Jo assumed their host had provided.

"I will be expecting a detailed progress report at dinner," Frye said in clipped tones. Despite the threatening words, the commanding quality of his voice faltered. He sounded as if he needed to rest.

"It takes time to set things up and make sure it's all operating properly," Cam responded.

"I suggest you work fast, laddie. And remember, I'll be keeping an eye on your progress." Frye gestured toward two TV cameras mounted on the walls, then stepped out of the room.

Despite the cameras, Jo breathed a heartfelt sigh of relief when the man had left. Until that moment she hadn't realized how deeply being in Frye's presence affected her.

She wanted to wrap her arms around Cam and bury her face in his shoulder to shut out the men and the bright lights. Instead she gave Donnel and his companion a quick assessment. Dressed in identical white T-shirts and black slacks, they were both fit, muscular and alert. The only noticeable difference was that Donnel had a thick head of hair, and his buddy had completely shaved his head.

It gave her a tiny feeling of control to assign him a name. Baldy stationed himself by the door, the gun still in his hand. Donnel holstered his weapon, and Jo wondered if she could grab it. Almost as quickly as the idea surfaced, she discarded it. Before she got into firing position, the other man would nail her.

Donnel pointed toward a chair in the corner. "Sit down and stay out of the way."

"No," Cam objected.

"The boss gave orders," Donnel rasped.

"She's been cooperating closely with me on the project. I can work twice as fast if I have her help setting things up."

Jo struggled not to look startled. She'd spent almost no time in his lab, and until a few days ago she hadn't even known about the wave compressor. However, she stood and walked over to one of the monitors.

"We got our orders," Donnel insisted, his hand resting on the butt of his pistol.

"I suggest you confer with Mr. Frye," Cam said in an even voice, as if he were the one in control of the situation. She flashed him an admiring look.

The two men exchanged uncertain glances. "We're not—" Donnel began.

Baldy cut him off and turned to Jo. "Okay, you can work with the professor. But no talking."

"I have to give her some directions," Cam shot back.

The man looked unhappy but didn't reply, and Jo wondered why he didn't consult his boss. Had Frye given orders not to be disturbed? Did he need to rest in the late afternoons? That would fit with his physical condition. Maybe they could use that to their advantage.

"Where are the lab coats?" Cam demanded.

"In the closet." Baldy jerked his hand toward a door in the far wall.

Cam strode to it, found two white coats and handed one to Jo. Gratefully she pulled it on and covered the revealing dress she'd been forced to wear for the scene in the dungeon. The sleeves were too long, so she rolled them up.

Cam's gaze burned into hers. "We haven't got much time."

She nodded tensely, responding to the double meaning of his words.

"I want you to make sure the cables to the monitors are plugged in tightly. Then check each one to make sure it's functioning properly."

"Yes." Checking the connections was easy enough, even for someone who'd gotten a *C* minus in high school physics. Then she supposed she'd just need to flip the power switches and fiddle with the contrast and brightness controls. She should be able to handle that.

She went down the row of machines, dutifully checking cables. One didn't seem to fit properly. "Cam, could you help me out?"

He didn't respond, and she swung around to see what he was doing. He was standing in the middle of the room, holding a small screwdriver in his hand.

Fear leapt inside her as she took a good look at him. His body was still as a statue and an utterly blank expression filled his face—as if there was no one at home behind his eyes.

Chapter Fourteen

A sensation of freezing cold crawled down Jo's spine as she stared at his stiff posture and the spaced-out look on his face. "Cam?"

Still, he didn't move, didn't respond.

"Okay, professor. Quit being cute." Donnel walked rapidly toward him and whacked him on the shoulder.

"Stop it," Jo shouted, rushing to her husband's side and grabbing the guard's arm. He shook her off, but he didn't hit Cam again.

"What's the matter with you? Huh?" Donnel demanded.

Anxiously Jo closed her hand over Cam's. It felt warm and dry. But he looked like a man who'd been put into suspended animation by a wicked witch. Lord, what had happened to him? Her heart blocking her windpipe, she took him by the shoulders. "Cam, what is it? What's wrong?"

The room was absolutely quiet as long seconds stretched.

"I'm going to call Frye," Baldy muttered, striding toward a wall panel. Opening it, he reached for the phone inside.

Before he could dial, Cam gave a little start as if he'd suddenly been awakened from a nap. His gaze swung to Jo, and she would have sworn there was someone else behind his eyes, focusing on her with laser intensity. His lips moved. No sound came out.

Frightened, she backed away.

Beads of moisture stood out on his forehead as if he was fighting some tremendous internal struggle. Then he seemed to come back to himself. "What's going on? Why the devil is everyone staring at me like I have two heads?"

"You stopped moving," Jo managed.

"Don't be idiotic. I was simply going to fix, uh..." He closed his mouth abruptly and looked around the lab, his attention focusing on the printer at one end of a long table. Then he glanced down at the screwdriver still clutched in his hand. "I was going to fix the paper drawer," he said with deep conviction. "Did I?"

"I don't know," Jo said.

"You didn't," Baldy answered. "You turned into a statue when you got halfway across the room. You sure you don't have epilepsy or something?"

"Epilepsy?" Jo and Cam both asked.

"My cousin's got it," Baldy informed them. "Used to have them, uh, petit mal seizures, they call them, before she started fallin' down on the floor and havin' a fit. She'd be talkin' to you, and all of a sudden it was like she was off in outer space or something."

Jo pressed her fingers over Cam's. "Nothing like this has ever happened to you before?" she asked. "I mean—"

"Of course not!" He cut her off sharply, but he sounded as if he wished he were absolutely certain.

"Get back to work," Donnel growled, "before we all get into trouble." He glanced meaningfully at one of the TV cameras.

"I was going to ask you to help me with this cable." Jo gestured toward the machine where she'd stopped working. "Could we do that before you fix the drawer?"

Cam followed her over to the apparatus.

"Are you really all right?" she asked as she leaned close to him, her shoulder against his.

"It's been a hell of a day. I'm, uh, probably just tired," he answered. "Maybe I fell asleep on my feet."

"Maybe you're having a flashback from the tranquilizer."

"You two, no personal conversation," Donnel warned. "Or she goes back in the corner, and I tell Sir Douglas you ain't cooperating."

Jo shut her mouth, but she kept a worried eye on Cam as he wiped the back of his hand across his forehead. Then he tightened the cable.

She wanted to press her fingers against his neck and feel his flesh against hers while she checked his pulse. Actually she wanted to pull him out of the room and wrap him protectively in her arms. Both of them had been unconscious for hours this morning, and then he'd had to pack up the equipment by himself and drive part of the way here. He should be in bed instead of setting up a laboratory. But Frye wasn't going to let him rest. He was going to push him unmercifully until he got the wave compressor working. Then he was going to kill them both. She had no illusions about their fate. Unless they could come up with some escape plan, they were history. Meanwhile, they had to look as if they were following instructions.

She and the guards kept observing Cam closely, but he had no more strange spells. So as she pretended to assist him, she began to think about how they could communicate in this fishbowl.

Knowing she was taking a terrible chance, she typed a short message on the screen. Then she called to Cam. "I'm not sure the computer is functioning correctly." Somehow she resisted the impulse to see if either of the guards was watching her. "Could you check something for me?"

Cam came casually over as if they were tending to routine lab business and looked at the screen, which she was shielding from the television camera with her body. On it she had typed, "Complex underground. One exit?"

He nodded thoughtfully and said, "I see what you mean. Let me find out if the software is working."

As he spoke, he typed, "Through garage. Careful of Frye. Dangerous."

"What about this?" Jo asked aloud.

The question she typed was, "Ventilator system?"

"Hey, what are you two up to over there?" Donnel called out, leaving his post at the door and striding toward them.

Jo's whole body went rigid. What if he saw the incriminating message?

Cam calmly touched a key that wiped the words from the screen. "The computer's not responding the way either one of us expected. There may be some bits on the hard drive that were damaged in the move. I need to run a diagnostic," he explained.

"You don't need your wife standing next to you, holding your hand."

Cam turned to Jo. "You can check the calibration on the wave oscillator."

Sure, she thought as she went over to what she hoped was the right machine. She sat down at the compressor controls. As the familiar wave pattern flickered on the monitor, a ray of hope opened in the blackness. The night she'd come down to the lab, Skip had been drawing energy from the machinery, and he'd used the power he absorbed to attack Cam.

He'd said he couldn't leave the house. But had Cam found some way to get him into the equipment before he'd packed it up? Could he somehow help them?

"You remember that anomalous phenomenon you got in the lab the other night?" she asked in a voice that she hoped sounded matter-of-fact.

Cam nodded.

Tension made her spine rigid. "Am I likely to get readings like that now?"

"I'm afraid that phenomenon is gone," Cam replied.

"Gone? How could it be gone?" she asked, her voice rising in disbelief.

"I have no control over—"

"That's enough." A familiar voice cut the air like a knife. The very air was suddenly charged with fear, as if a deadly gas had been pumped into the lab. Everyone turned to see Sir Douglas Frye standing in the doorway.

He gave Baldy and Donnel an assessing look that made them both cringe. Then his glittering gaze swung to Cam. "I hope for your wife's sake that you can show me some progress."

"It's taken us all of this time to set things up," Jo jumped in.

"Not good enough," Frye shot back.

"How do you expect him to work at top speed when you drugged him and then made him pack heavy machinery and drive out here? You're lucky he's functioning at all."

"No, you're lucky I'm so patient," Frye said in an even voice.

Jo steeled herself not to look away from his ruined face. But the visual contact did her very little good. His features had been distorted so terribly that she couldn't read his expression.

He surprised her by saying, "Maybe you're right. I was going to invite you to supper with me. But you might as well eat in your rooms and go straight to bed. We can start again at sunup."

"Rooms?" Cam asked.

"Yes. I learn from my mistakes. Unlike with Mr. and Mrs. Zacharias, I'm not going to give you the chance to discuss escape attempts while you're pretending to make love."

He turned and issued clipped orders to the guards. Then he left the room.

Jo locked her arms around Cam's waist and clung to him tightly, feeling the wild beating of his heart—and hers. Being separated now was like dying. She'd thought they'd have the night together. She'd thought she could tell Cam how awful she felt about the way she'd flung those horrid words at him and stamped off to the summerhouse. Now she wouldn't have the chance. Might never have the chance.

"I love you," was all she could whisper as she tried to shut out the knowledge that two sets of hostile eyes and a TV camera were watching the scene.

His lips moved against her ear so that only she could hear what he was saying. "I love you. More than my life."

"No. Don't say that!" She clasped him tighter, afraid of what his words meant.

Then his lips found hers, and she was lost in the desperation of the kiss. She put her heart and soul into it, trying to make him understand how much she needed him, and that life would mean nothing without him beside her.

Everything but Cam was wiped from her consciousness as she clung to him. It was a rude shock when a rough hand clasped her shoulder.

"I said, that's enough." Baldy's loud voice penetrated the insulating capsule she'd constructed around herself and Cam.

Jo blinked, realizing that the guard must have been speaking to them for some time. But she had heard nothing.

"Come on." He pushed her toward the room where she was to spend the night.

"Get your hands off her," Cam growled as he made a grab for Baldy. Donnel slammed him against the wall.

"Cam!"

Baldy pushed her away, and she landed on a narrow bed, panting. When the door slammed shut, she jumped up. But she was locked in. She looked frantically around the room. It wasn't the same one where she'd awakened. That had looked opulent. This one was more like a prison cell, with the cot along one wall and a toilet-sink combination on the other. Near the ceiling was one of the TV cameras that had become part of her life. She turned her back on the lens.

"Cam? Can you hear me, Cam? Are you all right?" she called urgently.

He didn't answer, and the silence was more than she could bear. She didn't even know where the goons had taken him. Or if he was all right.

She might have screamed out her anguish. Knowing that Frye was probably feeding on every detail was the incentive she needed to get control of herself.

With as much dignity as she could muster, she walked to the sink and washed her face and hands, concentrating on the simple activity as if it were the most important thing in her existence.

A slot in the door opened, dispensing a tray of food. Jo wasn't hungry. But she forced herself to sit down at the table and eat some of what tasted like a fairly decent beef-and-vegetable stew. At least prison slop wasn't part of Frye's torture.

But he must know that being separated from Cam was almost enough to make her unravel.

Except that she wouldn't. She was tough and fearless. Hadn't that been the crux of her stupid argument with Cam?

Her vision blurred. What an idiot she'd been to hurt him when he'd been trying his best to protect her.

It was several minutes before she could get herself under control. Then she focused on the simple task of choking down most of the food. Gradually she added another assignment—inspecting the cell's walls, the door... the ventilator ducts. They looked fairly large. Was there any chance of escaping through them?

What if the TV monitors were unmanned at the moment? What if she got the grate off and climbed into the shaft? She stopped in her tracks. What would Frye do to Cam if he found her missing?

Feeling icy cold sink into her bones, she yanked the covers aside, climbed into the bed and pulled the blanket up to her chin. Moments after she'd lain down, the bulbs in the ceiling dimmed slightly.

Was that automatic? Or was someone watching?

She couldn't close her eyes. Tension kept her body rigid and her mind racing. She didn't know how much time passed. Maybe it was hours later—or minutes—when she heard a strangled cry of pain.

She sat bolt upright on the bed and looked around. "Cam?"

He didn't answer, but she knew it was him.

Every nerve in her body tingled as she strained to hear something more. Seconds ticked slowly by. Then, "Jo. Help me." The voice was very weak, and it seemed to be floating toward her from the air duct.

Heedless of the camera, she leapt up. The grill was high above her head, and she ran back to get the table, shoving it across the room. Panting, she scrambled on top and peered through the vent, but there was nothing on the other side except blackness.

"Cam? Cam, answer me? Please."

All she could hear was the pounding of her own heart, and she began to wonder if she'd made up his voice out of her own fear and loneliness.

Straining her ears, she listened intently. A low moan reached her.

Grabbing the grillwork, she tried to shake the vent loose. But it was screwed tightly to the wall.

Looking around the room in desperation, she spotted the plate and utensils she'd set by the door. Of course there was no knife. But what about the handle of the spoon?

On the way back across the room, she stopped to glance at the TV camera. No one had come so far. Maybe they weren't monitoring her continuously. She might be out of range in the corner by the grill, but when they checked again, they'd certainly see that she wasn't in bed.

Quickly she fashioned the pillow and the blanket into a crude dummy and covered them with the sheet. It wouldn't pass a close inspection, but it was the best she could do.

Then she climbed back on the table and started working on the grill.

She could hear her own breath hissing in and out of her lungs as she worked frantically to unfasten the screws. What if this was all for nothing? What if she couldn't even fit into the vent when she got the covering off?

"Jo." His voice sounded closer now—and weaker.

She longed to tell him she was coming, but she didn't dare give herself away.

When she'd freed two screws, she grabbed the edge of the grate and pulled. The remaining fasteners came loose, and she had to catch herself to keep from falling backward. When she'd regained her balance, she set the grate on the table and stuck her head and shoulders through the opening.

At first she could see nothing in the darkness. Then she noticed a dim ray of light at the end of what appeared to be a rectangular shaft.

Very faintly, Cam's voice whispered in the darkness, calling her.

Her chest ached as she struggled to pull herself up and through the opening. Then she was lying prone on a cold metal surface. At least she didn't have to make a decision about which way to go. There was only one tunnel. Since it was too narrow for her to crawl, she had to slither along like a snake in a drainpipe.

Every time she reached a seam in the metal, it snagged and tugged at her dress and the skin of her legs. But she kept her lips pressed together and inched her way toward the opening at the end.

After what seemed like centuries, she reached the other grill. Beyond it she could see a cell identical to hers, only the bed was occupied—by Cam.

He had kicked the covers off the bed, and he was writhing and moaning as if he were in agony.

Her stomach twisted as she watched him from her high vantage point. Softly she called his name.

He didn't answer and she began to work on the grate as quickly as she could. With direct access to the clips that held the screws, she could push instead of pull. Minutes later, the grill came free, and she caught it before it clattered onto the floor.

Then she wiggled into the room.

Cam's body jerked as she climbed onto the bed and took him in her arms. She wanted to sob out her relief at being with him. She wanted to cling for dear life. She wanted to pour out her fear and her remorse. But she sensed that there was something terribly wrong, that she had to stay strong for him. "Sweetheart, what is it?"

His head sank to her shoulder, and he went very quiet—not the way he had this afternoon, but as if he were making a tremendous effort of will to keep still.

"Cam?"

She waited, her heart pounding in her chest. He needed a doctor.

She risked a glance over her shoulder at the TV camera, half expecting to hear heavy footsteps pounding down the hall. But nobody came. Either the guards were waiting to see what happened, or they weren't doing their job.

Cam pushed himself erect. When she reached for him again, his mouth twisted in a silent grimace, and his lids snapped open like window shades that had suddenly been released. The view beyond was utterly unexpected.

In that frozen second, mind-bending fear coursed through her veins. Dumbly she stared into the unfamiliar depth of his eyes, feeling as if she were sinking into quicksand. It was happening again. Like in the lab.

"You're not Cam," she gasped out as she backed away, even as she knew that the words were crazy.

"Skip," he wheezed.

"What?" Shaking her head, she tried to comprehend his meaning.

His hand shot out and locked around her wrist like an iron cuff. "Need help," he muttered.

"Ple-please . . . I—I don't understand."

His body jerked. "Jo? Oh, Lord, Jo." All at once his voice was suffused with an unimaginable depth of pain. "Hold me. If I lose you again, I'll lose my mind."

She still didn't understand. The only thing she knew was that Cam needed her urgently. She took him in her arms, rocking him and crooning wordless assurances.

When his hands came up to clasp her shoulders in a death grip, she felt the moisture in her eyes brim over and trickle down her cheeks.

"Please. You have to explain. What's going on? What's happening to you?" she whispered, drawing back so that she could search his face.

For heart-stopping seconds, he said nothing. Then he began to talk again in a voice so thin and strained that she had to focus all her attention on making the syllables into words. "Jo, Cam broke through for a few minutes. But now this is Skip talking to you."

"No. That's impossible."

"I'm with Cam. In his body."

She felt fear leap in her breast. For Cam. For his sanity. "Sweetheart, it's all right. You're going to be all right."

"I haven't gone soft in the head!" he persisted. "Pay attention to me! I know you're having trouble understanding what happened. But it's not Cam talking, and we don't have much time. They'll find out that the TVs are off and come in here."

"The TV—"

"Red, listen!" She went rigid at the sound of her nickname. For the first time she half believed what he was saying.

He continued rapidly, as if he expected to be cut off at any minute. "Cam brought me here—in his body."

"Skip couldn't leave the house."

"That's right. Not by myself. Before Cam loaded the equipment, I persuaded him to let me into his consciousness so I could help you."

"How?" she gasped.

"He absorbed my energy pattern—into himself. We were sharing his mind."

"He trusted you enough to let you do that?"

"No. But he went along with it. To save you. Then I did something stupid." He grimaced. "I got excited and started playing with his electrical equipment like a kid with a new set of model trains on Christmas. I should have realized that it could hurt him—that his body couldn't handle the overload. He passed out, and so did I, in a manner of speaking. When he came to, he thought I was gone—because I was still out of commission."

The explanation sounded insane. Yet as Jo stared at the man beside her, it made some sort of weird sense, if you granted the premise.

"Skip," she said softly, looking at him with new understanding. Even as she said his name, she wasn't sure she could handle this transformation.

He shuddered and reached for her, and it was a very strange sensation when he pulled her back into his embrace. With a low exclamation, he pressed her tightly against himself.

"Lord almighty, I've been watching you for weeks, wanting to touch you. I never thought I'd hold you again." He sighed, moving his cheek against hers, lifting his hands so he could winnow them through her hair. "Those red curls, I always loved the way they felt against my fingers."

She closed her eyes, and with the visual cues gone, she knew the truth. By the way he held her, by the subtle shift in his physical presence. All at once she could hardly deal with the mixture of emotions swirling through her.

"We had a fight," she whispered through the tears in her voice.

"Yeah, Randolph was real upset."

"No. I mean before Skip... before you were killed. I must be doomed to repeat my mistakes."

His body tensed.

She kept her eyes squeezed shut, because that was the only way she could feel she was really talking to Skip. "When you died, I never got a chance to tell you I was sorry."

"I knew. I saw you crying." In the darkness of the cell, he stroked her hair, giving her comfort and a kind of absolution. She sighed deeply. He continued speaking in a soothing tone. "The fight we had was as much my fault as yours. I didn't want any advice—or help. It's like a reversal of what's happening now between you and Randolph."

"What?"

"Back then I was the one who resented the words of caution when I thought I knew what I was doing."

The insight stunned her, more so because of the source. He'd just given her a very generous gift. My God, Cam had been trying to put a brake on her recklessness, just the way she'd been trying to save Skip. And neither she nor Skip had listened.

Did he regret his behavior as much as she? Was he here to make things come out differently? She clutched his shoulders. "Did you come back to try and take me away from Cam?"

Silence hung heavily in the air. "I didn't *come* for that. But once I got here it crossed my mind...." His voice trailed off.

She swallowed hard. "I appreciate the honesty."

"I may have done a lot of things wrong, but I could never lie to you, Red. At least give me that."

She felt a mingled sadness and relief. "Skip, things can never be the way they were. It tore me apart when you died. For a long time, I had to drag myself through every day. Then I met Cam, and I found out I wanted to live again. We had such a good marriage—a real partnership—until Frye started messing with us."

"And I came back—to add to the confusion."

She didn't deny the admission. It was a relief to finally speak honestly, to have things out in the open.

"I wanted you again, but I had enough sense to see I couldn't just step into your life."

"Thank you."

He swallowed hard. "I know how much Cam loves you. He'd give his life for you."

"I don't want him to do that!"

Skip started to say something else. Then his whole body tensed, and her eyes flew open.

"Red, we don't have much time. The guards are going to figure out I shut the TV sets off. I can help you. But there's something you have to do. You've got to tell Cam I'm here. You've got to make him understand that it's safe to let me take control again."

"In the lab this afternoon. Is that what happened to Cam when he looked so strange? You were trying to get out?"

"Yes. He fought me off. It was pretty dicey, sharing his consciousness with me. It damn near drove us both nuts. And he's fighting tooth and nail to keep it from happening again—even if he doesn't understand what he's doing."

She studied his face, wishing they could go back to the personal conversation, but knowing that if they didn't figure out a way to escape, nothing else would matter. "So how is it you're able to talk to me now?" she asked.

"When Cam went to sleep, I battled my way up to the surface. But it wasn't easy."

"You called me. Why didn't *you* come to *my* cell?"

He laughed. "Because Cam's shoulders won't fit through the ventilator duct."

Remembering the tight squeeze, she nodded. "Could we call the guards and have you overpower them?"

"No. I've got to be near the wave compressor. It's my source of energy. I need it to function effectively. And I need you to convince Cam you had a conversation with me. That you know I'm here."

"How? Frye's hardly letting us talk to each other."

"Yeah. That makes it rough."

She was silent for several moments as she tried to come up with some plan. "Can you read Cam's mind?"

"Yes. But I'm trying not to." He shuddered. "It's not pretty having a direct line to another person's most private thoughts. There's nothing you can hide."

She tried to imagine it. Every secret laid bare. Every emotion exposed.

"He wants to believe I'm gone. What we need is some kind of proof."

Jo racked her brain. "What if you give me some information neither one of us could possibly know?"

"You mean tell him about the time he was caught smoking behind Edmonson Mall?"

"Cam smoked?"

"He tried it when he was fourteen. But he wouldn't want you to know."

"Then we can't use anything like that. It has to be completely neutral." She snapped her fingers. "Do you remember when the three of us were talking about the laws of thermodynamics? Is there some formula or scientific jargon I could spout at him? Something I wouldn't know on my own—and he'd have to wonder where I got the information?"

"Wait a minute." His vision seemed to turn inward, as if he were listening to his own heartbeat. A moment later he said slowly, "Here's one of the most important thermodynamic equations—$dU = TdS - pdV$."

"$dU = TdS - pdV$," Jo parroted back.

"Can you remember that?"

"I hope so."

"All the quantities are a function of state," he droned. "For a change between two states, the integral of the equation will be valid even if the path is not reversible."

"Sure," Jo murmured before repeating the equation once more.

"Is there anything else?"

"You could try mentioning the Carnot cycle or the Brayton cycle."

"What are—?"

Skip clamped his hand around her arm. "The guards are talking about the camera. They've figured out it isn't functioning. They'll be down here in a minute to check on us."

Jo glanced frantically at the duct. "It took forever to climb in here," she gasped.

"Come on." He tugged her across the room.

"Wait." An idea struck her, and she twisted her fingers into her hair, freeing several bright red strands. "If Cam wakes up with these in his fingers, he'll wonder how they got there."

"Good thinking."

It was easier to get back into the vent with Skip boosting her up and giving her a shove down the narrow passage. "I'll pull it shut behind you," he whispered as she began to wiggle toward her own cell.

Trying not to make any noise, she moved down the metal duct as quickly as she could. But when she was only halfway to her room, she heard menacing footsteps thumping down the hall.

Chapter Fifteen

Jo froze. They were going to find her in here! They were going to pull her out by her legs and drag her to Frye.

Only the devil knew what punishment he'd think of.

She heard a key turn in the lock of her door. But before it could open, Cam started shouting. "Let me out of here, you bastards."

Except that it wasn't Cam. It was Skip. At least, she thought he was the one creating the disturbance as a smoke screen.

The footsteps retreated, and she heard a door clanging open. Not her door, Cam's.

"I demand to talk to Sir Douglas," the man in the cell bellowed.

"Take it easy."

Redoubling her efforts, she wormed down the duct, flopped through and lowered herself to the table. She had just enough time to slap the grate into place and push the table back when her own door opened.

A large, burly man filled the doorway. Grabbing Jo's arm, he slammed her back onto the bed. "What are you doing up?"

"I heard my husband moaning in his sleep. Is he all right?"

He looked at her suspiciously. "How did you disable the camera? What are you up to?"

"I didn't touch the camera. Is something wrong with it?"

"You mean it's just a big coincidence that the only equipment failure we've had in months comes when you're up to something?"

She shrugged. "I'm not responsible for your equipment. Please, I need to know about Cam. Is he hurt?"

"You don't need to know anything."

The man stomped out of the room, pulling the door closed behind him, leaving her shaking on the bed. She glanced up at the air return duct. One of the screws looked as if it was about to fall out, but she didn't dare climb up again and try to fix it, because she could be pretty sure that the guards were sitting at their posts glued to the TV monitors. And they would be for the rest of the night.

CAM WOKE WITH a terrible headache and the feeling that he'd been up half the night, although he knew that had to be his imagination. He'd had a hell of a day, and he'd conked out almost as soon as his head had hit the pillow. The only thing he could remember was a couple of weird dreams. In one of them Jo had been in here— in his cell with him. They'd talked, and he'd held her in his arms on the bed. What a case of blatant wish fulfillment, he thought with a snort.

He looked toward the stone wall across the room. He thought Jo was in the next cell. But he couldn't even be sure of that. Maybe he could communicate to her through the ventilator.

He rolled over on the narrow bed and tried to stretch the kinks out of his body. Some kind of threads were tangled in the fingers of his left hand. Puzzled, he brought the hand in front of his face and struggled to process what he was seeing.

Wound around the fingers were curly red strands of hair. Like Jo's.

He rubbed them back and forth against his fingertips, straightened them out and watched them snap back into their original curls. It had to be Jo's hair. Yet it couldn't be.

In the dream, just before she'd gone back to her own cell, she'd pulled several hairs from her head and pressed them into his hand. Or was he making that up?

He closed his eyes, straining to remember how she'd come to him in the night. The air duct. So that's how he'd gotten the idea of using it to communicate.

His eyes flicked to the grate. Was it really screwed into the wall? Or had he shoved it back into place after she'd left?

It was bizarre to be sifting through the details of a dream as if they were real. Yet the more he thought about them, the more solidity they assumed. And he had the physical evidence in his hand.

Unfortunately there was another way to explain the whole experience. He remembered the horror stories Jason had told him about Frye. What if the man were playing some of his famous mind games with him? Broadcasting "dreams" to him and leaving some of Jo's hair as a finishing touch?

Maybe she could tell him what was going on. He was about to push the table across the room when a voice blared from a hidden speaker. "Good morning, Dr. Randolph. You look as if you slept well. Fresh clothing has been provided. Be ready for breakfast with Sir Douglas in fifteen minutes."

He'd forgotten all about the damn camera spying on him.

Casually he glanced down at his fingers. Probably no one would realize he'd been looking at Jo's hair—if that's what it was. Still, he slipped the strands into his pocket as he walked toward the sink.

He washed, shaved and changed his clothing expeditiously. The underwear, slacks and shirt that had been provided fit perfectly, making him wonder again how long Frye had been planning the kidnapping.

When the door clicked open, he strode forward. Jo was standing a little way down the hall, and he was vastly grateful that Frye had let her put on something normal like jeans and a sweatshirt instead of the theatrical white dress of yesterday. She was with a guard he didn't recognize. As soon as she saw Cam, she pushed past her keeper and sprinted toward him.

Seconds later they were in each other's arms, clinging tightly.

"Are you all right?" they both asked at once.

"Yes."

His throat tight with emotion, he leaned back so he could inspect her face.

Her features were tense, her expression urgent. "I have to tell you about—"

"That's enough." One of the guards pulled her away.

"Take your hands off her."

The man's response was a mild, "I don't think either one of you wants to keep Sir Douglas waiting."

Hungry for contact, Cam kept his hand linked with Jo's as the escorts marched them down the corridor. And she clung to him with an iron grip.

"In here."

They were ushered into a small dining room that was a lot different from the cell where he'd spent the night. It looked as if it had been transported directly from a baroque mansion. Set into the stone walls were narrow stained-glass windows with lights behind them to give the illusion that they were illuminated by morning sunlight.

As if they had been invited to a formal brunch, Jo was escorted to the chair at one side of an elaborately carved mahogany table. Cam moved around to the other side.

A door in the paneling opened, and the man with the ruined face stepped through. Once again Cam steeled himself not to react.

"I trust you slept well," Frye said, keeping up the pretense that this was some kind of social occasion.

"Wonderfully." Cam matched his host's casual tone, but every sense was alert. He waited while a servant poured coffee and took orders.

"I trust you will be able to make more rapid progress on your wave compressor this morning," their captor picked up the conversation.

"I want some guarantees before I proceed," Cam answered, as if he had some maneuvering room.

Frye steepled his hands. "Such as?"

"I want you to let Jo go before I do any more work."

"Impossible. She knows too much."

"Then she'll know too much when I'm finished."

"Not necessarily. I assure you've heard from your friend, Mr. Zacharias, that I've been a keen student of mind-altering techniques. I believe I can erase the memory of this visit from her consciousness before she leaves."

The hairs on Cam's scalp prickled as he thought about Frye conducting some crippling mental experiment on Jo. "No."

"I'm afraid that's the best I can offer. Really, it's quite a safe technique. You'll be very pleased with the results."

"You think I'm going to take your word for that?"

"You don't have much choice."

"I can refuse to cooperate."

"That would be very unwise."

Jo leaned forward. "Do what he says so I can get out of here," she said in a strangled voice.

He studied her face. She looked frightened, except for her eyes, which bore into his as if she were trying to give him a subliminal message.

"I was practically pulling my hair out last night trying to come up with some new approach for your experiment," she said.

That got his attention. He held up his left hand and stared down at it.

She nodded almost imperceptibly.

Frye, who seemed to be unaware of the silent exchange, laughed. "Have you suddenly turned into a physicist, Mrs. Randolph?"

"Discussing my work with her is often very helpful," Cam answered.

"Yes. Do you remember those thermodynamic principles you and I and that lab assistant—what was his name, Skip—were discussing?"

"Skip?" Cam asked. "What about Skip?"

"He's here. In spirit."

Cam stared at her, unable to believe she knew what she was talking about.

"I mean, last night I was thinking about that formula he showed me for a change between two states." She spoke as if they were two graduate students having a casual conversation in the MIT cafeteria. "$dU = TdS - pdV$. Isn't the integral of the equation valid even if the path is not reversible?"

"Yes." Cam wondered where in the heck she'd picked up that bit of esoteric information. Was she implying Skip had somehow told her last night? It was an interesting theory, except that Skip knew as much about physics as she did, which was basically nothing at all.

"Well, I was wondering if you could couple that with a Brayton cycle, and maybe effect some change in your wave output."

He realized he was holding his spoon in a death grip and set it down with a thump on the table. "That might work."

Jo looked at Frye. "I'd like to assist my husband in the lab again today, and be allowed to discuss the experiment with him. Together we might be able to accomplish something important."

As the disfigured man considered the request, Cam struggled to keep his breathing even. *God, let her stay with me,* he prayed silently.

"All right," Frye finally said. "But I will be keeping a close eye on your activities through the television monitors. And if I detect any signs of duplicity, you will be sorry."

ON THE WAY to the lab, Jo clutched Cam's hand again, half-afraid that Frye was going to change his mind and have her dragged away, after all. But the door closed behind them and the guards, just as it had the day before.

Her heart thumped wildly in her chest as Cam began to turn on equipment. She was acutely conscious of the two men looking on. Frye must have selected them for their temperaments. Both of them looked less friendly than Donnel and Baldy—and *they* hadn't exactly been "Comedy Store" material.

If she only had two minutes alone with Cam, she could tell him so much. But at least she had a plan that might make him understand.

"Remember the evening I came down to help you in the lab, and you were picking up the anomalous energy matrix?" she asked.

He swung around to face her, his face quizzical. "I remember it very well."

"Didn't the machinery pinpoint the location of the *S* waves?"

"Yes," he said slowly. "*S* waves."

Jo nodded encouragingly. There were no *S* waves. But there was an anomalous energy matrix named Skip.

"Well, what if we rig up an, uh, *S* wave locater and check out this facility?" she continued with the scientific mumbo jumbo. "We may be able to discover the most favorable spot for the compressor."

She watched Cam stroke his chin. The guards eyed them suspiciously but didn't interfere.

Checking the supplies in the lab, Cam got out an electrical meter and hooked it into his system. Then he switched on the power. Immediately the auditory output began to chatter. The reading didn't change as he moved around the room. He gave Jo a direct look. "It's not working."

"Let me do it.'

"What's the difference who—?"

She lifted the wand out of his hand. "You stay there." As she moved away from him, the sound level decreased. When she moved back toward Cam, the readings began to accelerate again.

"Do you see what's happening?" she asked, tension making her voice thick.

"Every time it comes near me, it starts going crazy," he muttered.

She was watching him study the readout when the door burst open.

Whirling, she was in time to see Frye stalking into the laboratory.

The guards snapped to attention.

Frye ignored them as he glared at Jo.

"Permit me to answer the question. Your ludicrous little experiment amounts to a codswallop. You're not doing anything but wasting my time."

Jo cringed away from the steel threat in his voice. "Please, we—"

He cut her off with a chop of his hand and a look that could have shattered glass. "Or are you using some private code to transfer information? Is that it? I checked my records. You may be pretending your husband has a lab assistant named Skip, but no one by that name has been at your house for the past two months."

"Not at home. At Randolph Electronics," she answered.

"Stop lying to me! I have access to the Randolph personnel records. The only person named Skip who works for your husband is a file clerk." He gave both of them a dark look. "I knew there was something fishy about that performance you were putting on this morning at breakfast. Now I've given you enough rope to hang yourselves."

"You're wrong. We're trying to get the energy compressor working so I can get out of here," Jo said.

"You may be trying to get out of here, but your plans don't have anything to do with your husband's research. You think I know nothing about the process? I've studied the literature. I know more about it than anybody besides your husband and Jim Crowley. In fact, I'm the one who suggested the line of research to him."

"You?" Cam asked.

"Yes. After I got him interested, I offered to share the profits. He thought the money he got from me was just a downpayment."

While Jo struggled to digest that new piece of information, Frye kept talking to Cam.

"I think you need to be convinced that I am deadly serious about securing your cooperation." He turned to the guards. "We are going to level two of this operation."

The men immediately sprang into action. One of them grabbed Jo's arms. The other apprehended Cam. Frye pressed a button by the door, and one wall of the laboratory slid back, revealing a room that looked very much like the dungeon where Jo had been chained the day before.

It had been waiting there for her all the time.

"No!" She shrank away, but the guard who was holding her dragged her inside. Although she kicked and struggled, she didn't have a chance against the weight lifter who had her in his grasp.

When he buckled cuffs on her wrists and spread her arms, she couldn't keep herself from crying out. In the next moment, she wished she had been able to contain her fear.

Cam pulled himself from the other goon's grasp and lunged forward. "Stop it."

She watched helplessly as the man grabbed his shoulder, spun him around and landed a ham-size fist on his jaw.

Cam staggered back and hit the wall opposite hers. Somehow he recovered enough to land a punch of his own.

It did him little good. Once she was secured, both guards were free to go after him. One slammed a fist into his stomach. The other hauled him backward and cracked his head to one side.

Cam gasped. Jo screamed and fought to get loose as they fastened him the way they had her—with his arms stretched wide.

He slumped forward, and she cringed as she imagined the pain in his arms.

Frye stepped forward and cupped a hand under Cam's chin. "I'm through handling you with kid gloves. Your wife will not leave this room until the wave compressor is in working order. And the treatment she receives will be tied to the progress you're making."

Cam lifted his head. "You bastard."

Frye ignored the curse. "I'm going to have some lunch now, which should give you some time to contemplate your wife's vulnerability—and your own."

He strolled out of the room, and the wall closed behind him.

Chapter Sixteen

Jo gazed across at Cam, seeing the anguish on his face and the cuffs that bound him to the wall. The room was small. Perhaps he was only a dozen feet from her. But they might as well have been separated by the Grand Canyon.

Cam struggled against his bonds with terrible determination, and she could see that he was hurting himself.

"Don't," she cried out. "Your arms."

He stopped pulling against the restraints, but he stared at her with such pain in his eyes that she had to look away.

"I love you, Jo. I'm so sorry I got you into this, sweetheart."

"No. I should never have stamped out of the house like that."

He shook his head. "It's my fault. I'm supposed to have a business to run, but I never could resist playing inventor. I should have had the sense not to start fooling around with that damned wave generator. I should have known Crowley's offer was just too good to be true."

"You had no way of knowing Frye suggested the project. That he was using you to refinance his empire."

"If I'd—"

"Don't beat yourself for something you couldn't predict," she admonished, cutting him off. "We may not have much time, and we have to talk." She glanced at the camera on the wall. "Is he listening?"

"You mean, are we his luncheon entertainment? I don't know. He could be tuning us in now. He could be taping us for later viewing enjoyment."

"Oh, God, Cam."

"Pretend he's not there."

She wanted to do that with all her heart—to speak freely to her husband. But if she handled things wrong, Frye would come charging through the door and drag one of them away.

"Cam, let's concentrate on what's important." She leaned forward, aching to touch him, but the cuffs stopped her. So she caressed him the only way she could—with her gaze. Then she waited for a breathless moment, focusing his attention.

He nodded almost imperceptibly, and she plunged ahead. "I love you, and I know you didn't want anyone to find out your secret—that you're suffering from a split personality."

She rushed on past his startled exclamation. "Please. We have to talk about it, about what having both you and Skip—two men in one body—has meant to me."

He was watching her warily as if he was afraid of where the conversation was leading.

"Cam, I know you're going to have trouble believing this, but while you were asleep last night I talked to Skip. He told me what happened after I was kidnapped. About the way you passed out when he took control.''

''He disappeared,'' he said emphatically.

''I understand why you want to believe that. But he woke me up, and I had a conversation with him,'' she repeated. ''I tangled some of my hair in his fingers.''

When he glanced at his hand, she knew he must have found the strands. Now the guards would know for sure she'd been in his cell. But she was past the point of worrying about that.

''I want to get in touch with the Skip part of you now. Let him take over.''

''How?''

She looked at him wistfully. ''I don't know how. He told me I had to convince you it was safe. Oh, Cam, if I could just hold you.'' Her arms jerked against the bonds, and she winced.

''Don't.''

He stared across the endless miles that separated them. ''I'd give my life to save you, sweetheart, if I could.''

Moisture blurred her vision as she watched his anguished face. ''It's all right, Cam. Maybe it's too hard. Maybe Skip didn't know what he was talking about.''

''No! I'm not going to let Frye do anything else to you.'' He closed his eyes, and his whole body went rigid with concentration. She saw him grimace as beads of sweat popped out on his forehead.

Agonizing seconds ticked by as she imagined Frye stomping through the door and demanding to know what was going on.

Cam's face twisted, and he opened his mouth as if he were going to scream, but no sound came out.

She wanted to beg him to stop torturing himself. She clamped her hands into fists and waited, the tension in her own body building to almost unbearable proportions. The worst part was that she could do nothing to help him—only watch his terrible struggle.

He moaned and the sound seemed to come from a deep pit of despair. When he found his voice, it was low and strangled. "I . . . can't."

"It's all right. It's all right," she repeated. "I love you. I know you're doing the best you can."

Tears brimmed in his eyes, in hers. They both leaned forward, but the restraints on the wall held them cruelly apart.

"I've failed you again," he whispered.

"No."

The way he looked at her made her feel her own vulnerability. She shivered, but she had already surrendered to the inevitable. "Whatever Frye does from now on has nothing to do with what's gone before—between us," she whispered urgently. "Cam, I didn't mean what I said yesterday when I was angry. We've had a good marriage. I want you to know that I've been so happy these past few years, that loving you was the best thing that ever happened to me."

His face was a strange mixture of pain and joy. "Jo, you've completed my life. Every week, every month we've been together has made me understand how much I was missing before I met you. Then things started getting all messed up, and I didn't know how to get back on track. And the worst part was that I couldn't protect you—the very thing I held most dear."

She felt her heart might burst. There was so much she wanted to pack into these precious moments in this cold cell. If this was her last chance to talk to her husband, then there were important things he had to know. But Cam didn't give her a chance.

His face suffused with pain. "Whatever happens to me, I can't let that monster do anything else to you."

"You've done everything you could—everything humanly possible."

"Not quite." He stood straighter, his jaw clenched, his eyes fierce, as if he were facing a firing squad without a blindfold. "If this doesn't come out right, you'll know I gave it all I had." Then he whipped his head back, cracking it against the stone wall with a loud *thunk* that reverberated through the small room.

Jo screamed as his body slumped forward. He hung unconscious from the rings in the wall.

"Cam!"

He didn't answer. Instead, his face contorted. His muscles jerked in painful spasms.

Watching in horror, she called to him again. He only writhed like a marionette with twisted strings.

Unable to take any more of his agony, Jo squeezed her eyes shut and turned her face away, her cheek pressing against the cold stone. He had done this in a last desperate attempt to save her. Tears leaked through her closed lids and slid down her face.

She felt a sudden rush of air in the room, as if the door had opened, and she looked fearfully toward the entrance. But she and Cam were still alone.

No, not exactly. She felt a hand wiping away the tracks of moisture on her face, heard the sigh of some-one's breath close to her ear. "Jo."

Her eyes opened wider. Cam was still slumped against the wall. As she watched, his body straightened, and he pulled his arms into a more comfortable position.

With a grimace, he tested his footing.

"Oh, God, Cam. Are you all right?"

His lips didn't move. The whispered answer came from right beside her. "Yes."

She shivered all over. "You—"

"Shh."

"Tell me you're all right."

"As good as can be expected, Red." It was Skip talking. Yet it was still Cam, too. A strange blend of the two men in her life—their souls merged in one body—and outside of it, too.

Cam was still across the room. At the same time, he was only inches from her. She had prayed she might feel his touch just one more time. She closed her eyes and sighed as she felt the tender gliding of his fingers against her hand, the gentle brush of his lips against hers.

"Your poor head," she murmured.

"I figured out I had to be unconscious."

She winced.

The buckle on one of her cuffs moved, then stopped abruptly. His gaze focused expectantly on the door. "Get ready. Company's coming. He must have been watching, after all."

The wall leading to the lab slid back. First the guards appeared, stopping on either side of the opening like military sentries. A moment later, Frye stepped into the dungeon and marched straight toward Cam. "What the hell are you doing, Randolph, trying to bash your brains out?"

Cam was looking past Frye, toward the lab. Trying not to be obvious, Jo craned her neck. She could see the reading on one of the screens pulsing the way they had the night she'd come down to seduce Cam. But that didn't mean Skip could control the energy as he had when he'd been free of an earthly body.

Frye grasped Cam by the shoulders and shook him roughly. "Answer me when I'm talking to you."

Cam's head turned slowly toward the disfigured man. "If I can't work on the wave compressor, you have no reason to hold Jo."

A shiver went through her body. His answer told her he needed to buy some time.

"Wrong. I have good reason to take out my wrath on her," Frye growled.

"She's an innocent bystander. She's never done anything to hurt you."

Jo held her breath, struggling to keep her anxious gaze away from the lab equipment. After all this, the ghost couldn't do what he'd promised.

"She has very poor taste in friends. Noel Zacharias, to be specific."

"You'd condemn her for that?"

"Shut up," Frye shouted. "When I'm through with you two, I'm going to send Mr. and Mrs. Zacharias an urgent message that will get them here in double time. When they see your bodies, they'll know what's in store for them."

Jo couldn't suppress a strangled cry.

Cam stared stonily at Frye. "I don't think so."

"There's nothing you can do to stop me."

"You're wrong. Your little show is over. And mine is about to start." His attention shifted to one of the guards. The man jumped as a lightning fork of electricity slithered across the lab and tangled around his legs.

He tried to scramble away; the electricity followed the movement as if it were a vicious dog going after an intruder.

"No. Get away from me!" he shrieked.

The forks of lightning branched out, catching the second man, as well. Transfixed in horror, Jo watched it dance up their bodies like tiny neon snakes writhing on a victim.

They both screamed, their limbs jerking uncontrollably as the energy pulsed. A great burst set them toppling to the floor where they rolled and clawed helplessly with their hands at the flickers of energy cracking over them. Tiny wisps of smoke rose from parts of their clothing.

"Stop it!" Jo heard herself scream. "Stop it! That's enough."

Abruptly the two men went limp, either stunned or dead, she didn't know which.

"What—?" Frye gasped as he stared at the still bodies.

"You're getting more than you bargained for out of the wave compressor," Cam growled.

Frye took a step back. Then he turned and ran across the room, heading for the bank of equipment. Heading for the power switch.

Jo gasped. If he reached the cutoff, the show was over.

He was inches from his goal when sparks shot out of the machinery like a fireworks display gone haywire.

Frye screamed in pain and fell back several feet, but he had tremendous perseverance. As Jo watched in helpless horror, he lunged forward again. His hand connected with the switch and pulled it down.

Immediately the sparks stopped popping. For a moment there was utter silence in the lab.

Frye straightened, sucking in large drafts of air. Then he turned and began to stagger back toward Cam, a revolver in his hand. "I don't know how you put on that show, laddie. But you'll pay for it," he spat out as he trained the gun at Cam's left knee.

Cam didn't move, except for the muscles of his face, which locked themselves into lines of rigid concentration. Jo saw beads of sweat pop out on his brow the way they had when he'd been trying to give Skip control.

Frye raised the gun. "Maybe if you beg for mercy, I'll work on your wife first."

Time seemed to stand still.

"Leave her out of this."

"Protective till the end."

"Not the end," Cam spat out as sprays of electricity shot from his fingertips.

"What—?" Frye gasped, his steps faltering.

The fragmented sparks resolved into twin streams that struck the gun from both sides.

Frye let out a bellow of pain and fear as he sent the weapon sailing across the room. In the next second, the electricity was all over him, crackling and popping across the surface of his body the way it had with the guards.

He staggered back and toppled to the floor, his arms and legs writhing and jerking as though they were being sprayed by a hail of machine-gun bullets.

"Stop," Jo screamed. "Enough."

"Not by half," Skip's voice rang out. "Not after what the bastard said he was going to do to you."

It wasn't until the smell of singed flesh drifted toward them that the electricity shut off.

Cam slumped against the wall, panting heavily, all the color washed from his face.

"Are you all right?" Jo called out urgently.

He didn't answer, but she felt the buckle on one of her cuffs loosen. With agonizing slowness, the fastener opened and she pulled her arm free, rubbing it against her middle.

Then the other buckle began to move. "No. I can do it," she called out.

Cam made no reply. As quickly as she could, she freed herself. Then she was across the room, holding Cam erect with one arm while she unfastened his right hand from the cuff. He leaned on her heavily as she worked on the other restraint.

Finally he was free, and she lowered him gently to the floor.

"Open your eyes. Talk to me," she pleaded.

"Can't," he mumbled, his speech slurred.

"Skip?"

Neither Cam Randolph nor Skip O'Malley answered.

Cam turned his head against her breast, his eyes closed, his breath ragged. It took on the rhythm of sleep, and she cradled him in her arms, rocking him gently. He'd put out a tremendous effort, but his pulse was beating strongly and his color was good. She took courage from that. Because much as she wanted to, she couldn't simply sit here on the floor holding him. They were still in a precarious situation. She'd seen five of the guards in this stronghold and several other people. She had no idea who else might be here and how loyal they were to Sir Douglas.

With gentle hands she eased Cam to the floor. Then she checked on Frye. He was dead.

Picking up the gun, she returned to the lab and found the phone she'd seen behind the panel. Praying that she could get an outside line, she called Jason's pager. He rang her back almost immediately.

"It was Sir Douglas Frye who kidnapped me," she began after a brief exchange of greetings. "He's dead, and Cam and I are in the lab he set up." With a sick feeling in her chest, she glanced through the doorway to where Cam lay on the stone floor. "Cam may need medical attention."

"Was he shot?"

"No. It may be like what happened in the lab when he got a shock from the equipment. You've got to hurry." She sighed in frustration. "But I don't have a clue about our location."

"I do, and we're only a couple of miles from the complex. I enlarged the pictures you took at the warehouse. The guy in the photographs is wearing a ring with Frye's crest. So I started checking locations where he set up bolt holes. This is the only place where there's been a bunch of recent activity. I'm standing by with a squad of FBI agents."

"I'll use the public-address system to tell the guards Frye is dead and federal agents have the complex surrounded."

"Tell them that if they come out with their hands up, they won't be harmed."

The plan worked. Forty minutes later Jason had the complex secured.

"I'm glad you were out there," Jo breathed.

He grimaced. "If you want me to quit Randolph Security, I will."

"What?"

"Frye went after you to get revenge on me."

"You're not responsible for his vindictiveness. I'm sure Cam won't accept your resignation." From the tight lines of his face, she knew it would take a conversation with his partner to convince him. But with Cam still unconscious that was the least of her worries at the moment. "He needs you to run things until he's better," she whispered, and then looked down quickly before he saw the fear in her eyes.

A few minutes ago, she'd reluctantly left his side so that a physician named Southwick who'd come along with the rescue team could check his vital signs. When the doctor finished, Jo tried to read his expression.

"I don't think it's a concussion. And his blood pressure is normal." He looked perplexed. "But his temperature is two degrees below normal. You said something about an electrical accident?"

Jo's mind scrambled for an answer. There was no easy way to explain what had happened. If she started talking about ghost and wave compressors and energy transfers, he'd check her into the psychiatric ward for observation.

Southwick gave a verdict on Cam before she had to come up with a plausible lie. "We'd better get him to the hospital for observation."

"No!" The exclamation came from the man on the stretcher.

Jo's gaze shot to his face, and she crouched over him. "Are you all right?"

"No hospital," Cam managed to say.

"But—"

"Home." He made a tremendous effort and continued. "Lab equipment."

Jo reached for Cam's hand and held it tightly, as if she could give him her strength.

"He's not in any condition to say what he needs," the doctor broke in.

Jo looked from Cam to Southwick. On the face of it, the physician was right. But they weren't making an ordinary medical decision. Cam was unconscious because using the wave compressor as a weapon had injured him. What if he needed power from it to mend?

"He's got to be where we can cope with an emergency. What if his blood pressure drops suddenly or his heart stops, for example?" the doctor said.

Jo shuddered, torn between scientific logic and intuition. In her soul, taking Cam home seemed like the right thing to do. Yet that might be signing his death warrant.

"All right," she agreed. "The hospital."

Cam grimaced and tried to say something. But the words never reached his lips.

Chapter Seventeen

Five frightening, frustrating nights later, Jo sat beside Cam's hospital bed, holding his hand and feeling as if their linked fingers were the only thing keeping her from slipping into an abyss—or maybe the only thing keeping him in this world. Anxiously she watched his face, praying that his unconscious mind was still anchored to his body.

Her heart squeezed painfully inside her chest. They'd been through so much over the past months. Now there was nothing she could do for him except sit by his bed and hope he knew she was there.

She smoothed her free hand across his brow, shivering as she felt his icy flesh. He'd never wakened. Never uttered more than a few strangled words since he'd lain on the stretcher at Frye's.

Over the past few days, Southwick had ordered every medical test he thought might give a clue to Cam's condition. A parade of specialists had trooped through his room, and the only thing Southwick was able to tell her was that Cam was getting worse—and nobody could say why.

She'd finally gathered up enough courage to ask the question she was dreading. "Is he dying?"

Southwick hadn't answered straight out, but his medical mumbling had left little room for hope. Only a miracle could save him.

She'd gone from feeling numb to angry to helpless and back to angry. And at last in the depths of her despair, she'd made a decision. The doctors and the hospital weren't doing Cam a damn bit of good. Maybe he had been right all along. Maybe he did know what he needed. She only hoped she wasn't too late.

She was aware of Southwick standing in the doorway, his manner several degrees more hesitant than when they'd first met. She turned partway around, barely acknowledging his presence.

"Mrs. Randolph, I'm sorry. We've done everything we can."

"It won't make him worse if I take him home, will it?"

"Won't you reconsider? We can keep him more comfortable here."

"I doubt whether he'll notice." Jo stood. "I'll take responsibility. I'm going to call the ambulance crew I've had on standby."

Was it her imagination? Did Cam give a little sigh, as if he were profoundly relieved or profoundly thankful that they were getting out of this place? She'd been living on tiny scraps of half-imagined reactions for days. She didn't know whether he was really responding to her or whether she was making it up.

The only people Jo had told the truth about Cam to were Jason and Noel. After the initial disbelief, they'd been totally supportive. And both of them had helped her make arrangements. But the final responsibility was hers.

The ride home took an agonizing thirty minutes. With her mouth so dry she could barely speak, Jo had Cam moved to a comfortable bed that had been rolled into the lab. His face was still pale and his breathing shallow. Yet now he seemed to be resting easier.

Southwick had wanted to set up an intensive-care unit in their home. But the only equipment Jo needed was the wave generator.

"Cam, I love you so much," she said when they were finally alone. "Am I doing the right thing?"

He couldn't answer, and she felt the weight of terrible responsibility pressing down on her shoulders. All the traumas of the past months were prelude. During the endless days in the hospital she'd had little to think about except how deeply she loved Cameron Randolph and how much she wanted to live the rest of her life with him. What she'd had with Skip was a different kind of relationship. She'd loved him unreservedly. But it had been the love of a young woman who'd been willing to let her husband dominate the marriage. That was her past. Cam was her present and future. They'd forged a love that was deeper, stronger than anything she'd known. And it was almost impossible to imagine going on without him.

But she'd felt him slipping away from her inch by inch. So she was going to do the only thing left that might bring him back—a continuation of the experiments he'd started in this lab. Only the whole thing could blow up in his face.

She squeezed his hand again. Her heart leapt when she thought she detected the hint of an answering contraction in his muscles.

With a mingling of fear and faith she crossed the room to the wave compressor and threw the power switch.

Jason had given her a duplicate set of Cam's notes. Murmuring a prayer for courage, she began to adjust the output to the setting Cam had used when he'd brought the ghost into focus. It was impossible to keep her fingers steady, and the readings jumped from one level to another. Blood roared in her ears so loudly that she felt as if she were going to faint. Every few seconds, she glanced back at the unconscious man, watching his eyes, his mouth, his expression. The color of his skin. Was he responding? And if this mad-scientist experiment did work, who would survive? Would she bring back Cameron Randolph or Skip O'Malley? She reached the power level indicated in Cam's notes, and nothing happened. After agonizing seconds, she turned the knob a few more notches.

Cam's eyelids fluttered.

Softly she called his name. But there was no other response. Her heart blocking her windpipe, Jo upped the voltage. This time, his muscles twitched, and his body jerked on the bed as if an electrical current were coursing through his cells. Then his face contorted in a terrible grimace and his lips drew back from his teeth, as if he were undergoing unbearable torture.

Frightened, Jo spun the dial of the wave compressor, and the energy level went down. Cam flopped back onto the mattress, his chest heaving as if he couldn't suck enough air into his lungs.

There was no other sound to break the deathly silence in the room. She darted to the bed and took him in her arms. "Oh, Cam, Cam. I didn't know. I'm so sorry."

For several pounding heartbeats, he lay deathly still. Frantically she pressed her fingers against his neck, feeling for a pulse. It was erratic but stronger than she'd anticipated.

When she raised her gaze, she gasped. For the first time in days, his eyes were open. He looked around the lab, then back at her.

"Cam?"

His lips moved, but the words that came out were too low for her to hear.

"I hurt you," she whispered, her throat clogged with tears.

His eyes swung to the wave compressor.

"I'll turn it off."

"No." The protest was the barest whisper in the silent room.

His eyes burned into hers, and she tried to read the message he was sending. "You can't want more of that," she breathed.

His whole body trembling with the effort, he nodded.

Did he really know what was best? She was so sick with dread that she felt as if she were going to throw up. She'd already turned up the power far higher than Cam's recorded settings. How much could he take?

Grabbing the end of the bed, she pulled him over to the machinery. Now she could reach the controls with one hand while she laced the other with Cam's. Anxiously watching his face, she began again, slowly increasing the power. This time his body reacted sooner. This time when his limbs began to spasm, she threw her body across his and hung on to him through the terrible ordeal.

"Jo." His voice was low and unrecognizable.

She was afraid to look up and meet his eyes. Afraid of what she might see.

"Thank you." His voice was stronger but still so thick she couldn't be sure who was speaking.

Somewhere upstairs she heard the sound of the grandfather clock chiming, and she paused to listen to the strokes. Twelve o'clock. The reckoning hour. The symbolism wasn't lost on her.

She felt the man on the bed waiting for her to raise her head. Pushing herself up on trembling arms, she looked into his face. His gray eyes were filled with the intensity she'd come to recognize. "Cam."

"Yes."

"Oh, thank God." The horrible tension inside her exploded into a series of racking sobs. Her body shook uncontrollably, and all she could do was cling to him and let the joyful weeping take her where it would.

It was his hands stroking through her hair that finally calmed her. Gradually she relaxed in his embrace. Both of them shifted to a more comfortable position on the bed.

She'd thought she'd never cuddle against him like this again. Thankfully she rubbed her cheek against his shoulder. "I've got you back."

"You saved my life."

"I was so scared when I took you out of the hospital. I could have been bringing you home to die."

"I'm feeling a hell of a lot better now."

She could see that it was true. His color was back to normal, and she could feel the strength in his arms as he held her.

"What happened to you?" she asked quietly.

"Those fireworks at Frye's took a lot out of me."

"I was afraid you'd given your life to save me."

"I would have."

"Oh, Lord, Cam, letting Skip take over like that was the bravest thing I've ever seen anyone do."

"*My* life wouldn't have meant anything without you."

"It's over now."

"You did the right thing, bringing me home. I needed the wave compressor to get my mind and body back in—in sync—I guess you'd call it."

"How did you know?"

There was a long hesitation. "Skip explained it to me."

She raised up to look at him.

He tangled his fingers in her hair again, as if he were shifting priceless coins through his fingers. "After the ruckus was over, Skip could have gone back where he came from, but he stayed with me," he said. "If he hadn't, I might not have been able to hold any kind of connection between my mind and body. He could have let me self-destruct. He didn't."

"I'd like to thank him for that and for everything else he's done," she breathed.

"You can."

"What do you mean?"

"He's still here."

"You're— He's listening to this conversation?"

"Does that make you uncomfortable?"

She turned aside the question. "I thought you couldn't deal with him in your mind."

"I had to—if I wanted to save you from Frye." His Adam's apple bobbed. "He and I have come to terms with each other. When we first merged, it was agony for both of us. We have complete access to each other's consciousness. There's nothing we can hide from each other. Nothing. He knows every secret I've buried from the world—and my deepest emotions, like the way I felt when I found you lying on the pavement.''

She tried to imagine that kind of intimacy. The idea was staggering.

''I know how he reacted when you first walked into his office, and what it was like when he got shot and died.''

Jo gasped.

''It's all there. The good, the bad, the shameful, the exalted.''

''How do you feel about him now?''

''He's my guest—for want of a better word. And even when he leaves, I'll still have all his memories. I'll always know that when he was killed, the worst part for him was not getting to say goodbye to you.''

''Oh!'' The exclamation was a strangled cry.

''You have a second chance.''

Moisture blurred her vision as she tried to comprehend not just his words but the implications behind them.

''Jo, it isn't just sharing consciousness that unites us. It's loving you. Without that, we never could have merged.''

Transfixed, she gazed up at him, mesmerized by the mystical light flickering in his eyes.

''I love you. I've loved you for a long, long time,'' he said, his fingertips gliding over her face with gentle wonder.

Her breath stilled as his lips followed the course his fingers had charted. When he reached her mouth, a tremor went through her.

''Jo?''

She raised her arms and circled his neck, feeling the muscle and sinew of his body. This was Cam, her husband. His mouth, his body—so dear, so familiar. Yet she knew he had spoken the truth. He was more.

"Oh, Jo." He sighed. "Jo." His mouth took gentle possession of hers. Her lids drifted closed as she tasted him, stroked his tongue. As he felt her consent, the kiss deepened, his mouth wet and hot as it devoured hers.

The blood pounded in her veins. She was drowning in the taste, the scent, the feel of him. She'd been afraid they'd never do this again. Now here he was in her arms.

He pulled back far enough to gaze down at her. "There's something else."

Light flared in his eyes, igniting an answering spark deep within her.

"If we make love tonight without using protection, we can make a baby."

They hadn't discussed children since the day he'd brought up the subject. But as she looked into his eyes, she knew how much her feelings about having a family had changed. She loved Cam so much and she wanted to give that gift to their children. She sent him a slow smile that she hoped conveyed everything in her heart. "You're sure of that?"

He let out the breath he'd been holding. "You've changed your mind."

"Yes. About a lot of things. After what I've been through, I don't have to prove my courage. I can concentrate on what's important."

"There's nothing like thinking you're going to die to help you get your priorities straight."

"Like starting a family. How do you know we can conceive tonight?"

"When . . . I . . . look at people, I see an aura around them. Yours is different, tonight. Here." He gently glided his palm across her abdomen.

Her breath caught in her throat. For an eternity of heartbeats, neither one of them moved.

"It's your call. We don't have to do anything about it unless you want to."

She covered his hand with hers. "I want to."

He took her lips again. And she cupped her palms around his face, accepting all the love he embodied. Accepting everything he offered.

He smiled down into her eyes. Then his hands began to drift over her arms, making the fine hairs there stand on end. She felt as if little shock waves of electricity were playing over her skin. When she looked, she saw a drift of tiny blue lights trailing after his fingertips.

"Oh!"

"Umm. Feels good." He grinned. "We're making sparks."

She gazed at the effect in wonder, even as she opened herself to the sensation transmitting itself from his hands to her body. It was arousing, yet it was like a mystical blessing, binding them together.

"I think I'd like a little more skin to play with."

"I think that can be arranged." She reached for the buttons at her neck.

He stopped her. "Let me."

Her breath caught as he slowly inched her shirt up and over her head. Then his hands slid against her heated flesh and dispatched the catch of her bra. Lifting her hips, she kicked off her sweatpants and lay naked beside him.

His gaze traveled over her, slow and hot, making her insides melt. She might have lifted her hand to cover the scar on her breast, but she kept her arms at her sides.

"Jo, you're the most gorgeous thing I've ever seen."

His voice was so thick with emotion that she felt her skin glow all over. Reaching out, she tugged at the hem of his shirt, getting it out of her way so she could flatten her hand against his chest and feel the beating of his heart.

The moment was so laden with mystery and promise that she struggled to breathe in and out.

"I know," he whispered. "I know."

Silently they removed the rest of his clothing. When he was as naked as she, he gave her a slow smile that warmed her from the inside out.

He gazed down at her for a long moment. Then he did it again—that clever trick he'd acquired. His fingers sifted through her hair, stirring a cloud of little sparks around her head.

"Oh!"

"You look like a fairy princess." He grinned, obviously pleased with his supernatural powers. Slowly his hands moved down her body, over her breasts, to the juncture of her legs, setting off tingling bursts wherever he touched and stroked.

Little gasps of pleasure rose in her throat as each tiny electrical charge transferred itself from his body to hers, suffusing her in a glow of arousal that was almost too much to bear.

"I wish you could feel what I'm feeling. I wish I could do that to you," she cried out.

"Try it."

She raised her hand, stroking it along his cheek. Tiny pinpoints of white light trailed from her fingers like newly made diamonds, and she stared at them in wonder.

He turned his face to kiss her palm, the buzz of electricity like the hum of honeybees against her flesh.

They shared the power. She moved her hands over his body, reveling in the pleasure she gave him—and the way it came back to her in an almost mystical exchange of energy.

The rich mixture of sensuality and spiritual communion went on for a long time, building and building to impossible heights, as multihued points of light danced around them like stars in a velvet night.

"Now."

They both spoke, both knew when it was time. Then his body was covering hers, sinking into hers, and she understood that everything that had come before had only been a prelude to something even more wondrous.

She gazed up at him in awe. The shimmering light was all around them so that she could no longer see the room or even the bed on which they lay. There was only this man, loving her with his body, his heart, his soul, as no man had ever loved a woman in the history of the world. Now she strove to give that joy back to him a thousandfold.

All of her senses were tuned to his with exquisite precision. They moved together in perfect rhythm, forming a bond that she sensed could never shatter. Not in this lifetime. Not beyond.

Her breath came in gasps as she neared the peak of fulfillment. She felt him shudder, felt his seed pour into her. Then she cried out as her own rapture took her.

Afterward she clung to him, coming slowly back to earth, drifting in his arms.

Her lips brushed his ear. "Your baby."

"Our baby."

Exhausted and exalted, she could only nestle against the warmth of his body, safe and secure.

A long time later he whispered, "I love you, Jo. I'll always love you."

She turned toward him, clutching his shoulders.

"It's time to leave." The bittersweet note in his voice made her lids blink open.

She understood it was Skip speaking now. "I'll always love you, too," he continued. "But our marriage was at a different time in your life. I can see how much you've grown and changed for the better. You were right. Things can never be the same."

"I'm glad you understand," she murmured.

"Cam is the right one for you now. Be happy, both of you."

Even as she held him tightly in her grasp, she saw a burst of starlight in the depths of his eyes, saw the supernatural aura fade.

Then Cam was holding her, cradling her in their marriage bed. She had never been more sure of his love.

"Part of him is still here." He touched his chest. "Part of him will always be with me—with us."

"We formed a bond."

"Yes. A bond of love."

INTRIGUE®

Are you a word sleuth? If so, find the hidden clues and help
Familiar the Cat solve his next caper in
FAMILIAR REMEDY by Caroline Burnes!
(Harlequin Intrigue #293, coming next month)

```
F  B  E  D  A  N  I  E  L  G  X  K  L  A
E  Q  U  A  R  Y  X  B  N  N  O  P  Z  T
L  U  F  N  S  V  H  M  C  S  X  R  W  F
I  L  J  G  M  A  N  Q  M  E  O  E  I  P
N  W  A  E  I  F  M  U  M  C  N  C  N  O
E  A  H  R  N  E  O  K  Z  R  S  Z  K  I
S  T  R  I  O  X  P  B  T  E  G  W  T  S
L  A  E  W  T  E  L  X  V  T  A  H  L  O
E  W  R  L  I  E  Y  P  A  S  S  I  O  N
U  C  E  A  D  F  H  R  I  T  E  T  V  C
T  J  T  S  H  Y  K  O  L  B  D  E  B  O
H  J  A  M  U  W  V  M  U  R  D  E  R  L
Z  D  C  Y  X  B  N  N  D  S  S  W  R  I
L  K  J  E  V  O  L  F  G  H  E  A  T  Y
```

CLUES:

FELINE SLEUTH	G-MAN	MURDER
SARAH	PASSION	SECRETS
DANIEL	CATERER	DANGER
POISON	SOCKS	LOVE
WHITE HOUSE	MEOW	

WDF-1

Answers

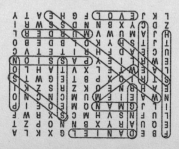

This summer, come cruising with Harlequin Books!

PORTS OF CALL

In July, August and September, excitement, danger and, of course, romance can be found in Lynn Leslie's exciting new miniseries PORTS OF CALL. Not only can you cruise the South Pacific, the Caribbean and the Nile, your journey will also take you to Harlequin Superromance®, Harlequin Intrigue® and Harlequin American Romance®.

- ◆ In July, cruise the South Pacific with SINGAPORE FLING, a Harlequin Superromance
- ◆ NIGHT OF THE NILE from Harlequin Intrigue will heat up your August
- ◆ September is the perfect month for CRUISIN' MR. DIAMOND from Harlequin American Romance

So, cruise through the summer with LYNN LESLIE and HARLEQUIN BOOKS!

CRUISE

HARLEQUIN®

I N T R I G U E®

Harlequin Intrigue
invites you to
celebrate

A Decade of Danger & Desire

It's a year of celebration for Harlequin Intrigue, as we commemorate ten years of bringing you the best in romantic suspense. And to help celebrate, you can RETURN TO THE SCENE OF THE CRIME with a limited hardcover collection of four of Harlequin Intrigue's most popular earlier titles, written by four of your favorite authors:

REBECCA YORK	Shattered Vows (43 Light Street novel)
M.J. RODGERS	For Love or Money
PATRICIA ROSEMOOR	Crimson Holiday
LAURA PENDER	Déjà Vu

This unique collection will not be available in retail stores and is only available through this exclusive offer.

Mail the certificate below, along with four (4) original proof-of-purchase coupons from one Harlequin Intrigue Decade of Danger & Desire novel you received in July, August, September and October 1994, plus $1.75 postage and handling (check or money order—please do not send cash), payable to Harlequin Books, to:

In the U.S.	In Canada
Decade of Danger and Desire	Decade of Danger and Desire
Harlequin Books	Harlequin Books
P.O. Box 9048	P.O. Box 623
Buffalo, NY 14269-9048	Fort Erie, Ontario L2A 5X3

FREE GIFT CERTIFICATE

Name:_____

Address_____

City:_____ State/Province: _____ Zip/Postal: _____

Account # _____   086 KCG-R

(Please allow 4-6 weeks for delivery. Hurry! Quantities are limited. Offer expires January 31, 1995)

A Decade of Danger & Desire

HARLEQUIN INTRIGUE
DECADE OF DANGER AND DESIRE
ONE PROOF OF PURCHASE   **086-KCG-R**